STAYING ALIVE

A POST-APOCALYPTIC EMP SURVIVAL THRILLER - THE EMP BOOK 2

RYAN WESTFIELD

1

GEORGIA

Georgia peered through the scope of her hunting rifle. There was a doe right in the crosshairs. It looked like it had some fat on it, which was good because food was scarce these days. Eating pure protein could kill you, and eating fat gave you more calories. That meant surviving longer.

It had only been two weeks since they'd arrived at the farmhouse, but their supplies were dwindling rapidly. They hadn't brought that much food with them. And there were six of them to feed. The canned food they'd found in the basement had turned out to be bad. Bacteria had gotten in.

Georgia's finger was on the trigger. She was about to squeeze it when she heard a noise off to her right.

She was already frozen, but she felt her muscles tense up with the sound. It was an eerie sound, too far away to tell what it was. It was slight, barely audible. The only thing she knew was that it didn't sound like an animal. It didn't sound like something natural. From all the time she'd spent hunting throughout her life, Georgia was well aware of the normal sounds of the forest.

There was another sound. This time it sounded like laughter. Human laughter.

Georgia's heart pounded in her chest. She didn't want to admit it even to herself, but she was scared. Perhaps terrified.

This was what they'd been fearing: other groups moving into the area. It had been two weeks since the EMP, and while many must have perished in the cities, there were certainly plenty who had survived. And now they'd be doing what was only natural and heading out into the rural areas. They'd be looking for food, space, and security.

And the ones who made it out of the cities would be the strongest, smartest, and most heavily armed. They posed the biggest threat to those who lived in the farmhouse.

Georgia was lying flat on her stomach, and she tried to make herself lie even flatter. Fortunately, she was wearing camo hunting gear, and she blended fairly well into the surrounding woods. She hadn't worn anything orange. Leaving for this hunting trip, she'd been well aware of the possibility of running into someone else. That was why she didn't want anyone else to come with her. The more people, the greater the risk of getting discovered.

For now, the safest thing for everyone in the farmhouse seemed to be to try to remain undiscovered.

But that would only work for so long.

The farmhouse was back quite a ways from the road. And the geography of the area made it difficult to discover accidentally while hiking through the woods.

Difficult, but not impossible. In fact, maybe it was easier than they'd assumed.

After all, there was that trail that Max, Mandy, Georgia, Chad, and Georgia's children had taken.

Sooner or later, someone would come along.

And that someone, or someones, would pose the biggest threat to their survival.

Now it looked like that time had come.

Georgia waited, frozen, trying to keep her breathing as silent as possible.

Soon, she heard footsteps and voices. They were moving towards her, whoever they were.

By the sounds, she guessed there were three or four of them. She could identify three distinct voices. They were male voices, harsh and loud. But she couldn't yet make out what they were saying.

Would they pass right by Georgia?

Her hiding spot was good, behind a rotten old log over which she held her rifle, but it wasn't good enough to conceal her if they were going to pass right by her.

The trees with their full green leaves blocked the men from Georgia's view.

Their footsteps were getting louder. Soon, she could hear their conversation.

"Did you see the look on his face?" one of the men said. His voice was callous and had a cruel tone to it.

"Damn, I've never seen someone like that. He should have taken it like a man."

"He was crying the whole time."

The men laughed.

"I hit him right between the eyes."

"It was a good shot, but I would have done better."

"How could it get any better than right between the eyes? Haven't you ever seen any movies?"

Georgia's mind was moving a mile a minute. These men sounded like cold-blooded murderers. And here they were, celebrating the pain and suffering they had caused. Part of her fear was turning to disgust.

Georgia was strong, and while she feared for the safety of her children, she wasn't going to let it overtake her. She would do what she had to do, whatever that was.

She could see the men now.

There were three of them, walking in a single file line through the woods. It seemed as if they'd pass by Georgia, but not run directly into her. With a little luck, they wouldn't spot her.

The three wore an assortment of clothing and gear. Judging by their conversation, Georgia guessed that they'd taken gear from their victims, slowly assembling their hodgepodge outfits.

One had a crude tattoo visible on his neck. Maybe it was a prison tattoo.

Two men had assault rifles. One was definitely an AR-15, with a scope on it. The other looked like an AK-47 knockoff, cheap and crude but still quite lethal. The third man had a handgun in a holster.

They outnumbered her. And they had considerably more firepower.

And it was too late to run. If she got up, they'd see her. Judging by their conversation, they weren't going to simply want to make friends. They weren't going to want to chat about the end of the world. They were, like everyone else, looking to survive, by whatever means necessary.

Georgia had a feeling that these men had survived so far by simply being crueler, and willing to take their "whatever means necessary" farther than most.

"I'm starving," said one of them, speaking loudly. He had a buzzed haircut and a gaunt face. "We're going to have to find someone with food soon. I'm tired of the food we've got."

"Maybe we can have some fun while we're at it," said his companion.

"Don't we always?"

The third one didn't speak, but just laughed deeply. It was an ominous sort of chuckle, low and rumbly.

With any luck, they wouldn't see Georgia.

But they were headed in the direction of the farmhouse. If they kept heading that way, it'd be almost impossible for them to miss it.

Georgia knew that someone would be on watch. When she had left, it had been Chad.

She just hoped that he'd kept his eyes open.

2

MAX

Max's leg was still hurting him, but he was doing better. Mandy kept telling him not to expect too much. After all, it had only been two weeks. "You're doing better than most people who've been shot," she'd said. "You got really lucky."

The bullet hadn't hit the bone. It'd been a good bullet wound, as far as bullet wounds went.

To everyone's surprise, including Max's, he was starting to hobble around the house with the aid of a makeshift cane. If the bullet wound had been anything more than minor, walking simply wouldn't have been possible for many more weeks, in the best circumstances. Still, it was incredible. He'd been lucky.

Max had been taking antibiotics to ward off a possible infection, and Georgia and Mandy had even helped him pack sugar into the wound. Sugar was an old trick used by field doctors when supplies ran short, and it worked well enough, sometimes even better than anything else.

"How you doing?" said Mandy, knocking on the already open bedroom door.

Max motioned for her to come in.

"What are you doing?" said Mandy. "You need to be in bed, resting."

"Exercises," said Max.

His face was sweaty with exertion. It took all his concentration to push beyond the pain. He was attempting body weight squats, an exercise that had never been harder for him.

"You need to be resting that leg," said Mandy. "If you want it to heal properly."

"This isn't the time for laying around in bed," said Max. "I need to be up and active as soon as possible."

"I don't know what you're so worried about," said Mandy. "Except for that body, we haven't seen anyone. You keep saying that people are coming, but no one ever does."

"Trust me," said Max, finishing his squat and nearly collapsing into a nearby chair. "They're coming. And the longer we wait without seeing anyone, the more intense the chaos in the cities must have been. Only the strongest..."

"Will get out alive... yeah, yeah," said Mandy. "You've said it a million times."

Tensions had been growing between Max and Mandy over the last two weeks. What had initially seemed like a budding romance had quickly imploded under the intense tensions inherent in the situation.

"What did you want to see me about?" said Max.

"It's the well," said Mandy. "There's no more water."

"What do you mean there's no more water?"

"I mean exactly what I said. It's simply not coming out."

Max didn't say anything. He'd been fearing this. Over the last week, the water had been looking murkier and murkier. And a day earlier, the water had been so off-color that they'd decided it would be best to purify it before drinking it.

"What are we going to do?" said Mandy. "The kids are worried."

Max nodded. "They should be worried," he said. "And to answer your question, I don't know yet."

"How can you say they should be worried? They're just kids. We need to protect them."

"There's no protecting them from what's happening," said Max. "At least not in the sense of shielding them from the reality around them."

Mandy didn't say anything. She simply frowned more than usual.

"I'm going to go check on the well," said Max.

He got up, somewhat painfully, from the chair. He hobbled past Mandy, who stared him down with her arms crossed in front of her.

Max weaved his way through the hallways of the old farmhouse. Even in the day, the hallways were dark. The wallpaper was peeling in places, and some of the floorboards were loose.

The stairs were tricky, but Max managed them.

As long as he kept using his leg, thought Max, he'd be recovered in no time. He didn't like to think about what would have happened if it had been a more serious injury. Max was sure that he himself needed to be active. He felt responsible for the others—without Max, they would be lost.

Max had set up a watch schedule. Max, Mandy, Georgia, Chad, James, and Sadie all took turns. Mandy had protested about including James and Sadie in the watch schedule, but everyone else was on board. Georgia was protective of her kids, but she recognized, unlike Mandy, that the better they were at taking care of themselves, the longer they'd survive.

James and Sadie were resting in the living room, their eyes barely open. Each lay on a separate couch, tired from their early morning watch shifts.

Max walked past them without greeting them. Better to let them rest.

Outside, the sun was shining brightly. A gentle breeze blew through the leaves of the trees. The grass was a brilliant green, and the forest beyond the farmhouse's lot looked inviting and peaceful.

But Max knew better than to be fooled by appearances.

Mandy seemed to think that everything was fine now that they were at the farmhouse. She'd thought all they had to do was figure out the drinking water situation, start growing their own food, maybe find a few animals, and everything would be fine.

Max knew better.

He knew people would be coming. The most vicious of the vicious. Those were the only ones who would be making their way in this direction. Sure, there'd be others, people like Max and Mandy. There were sure to be decent people who had survived.

The trouble would be figuring out who was who.

So far, there'd been no contact.

Georgia had come across one dead body in the woods. A man in his early fifties, gaunt with the muscle wasting that came with starvation. On first glance, he'd apparently died of pure exhaustion. But on closer inspection, Georgia had noticed that he was full of what looked like stab wounds. He'd simply bled out. Georgia had brought James and Chad back to the body, and they'd buried the man in a shallow grave.

"How's it going up there?" said Max, looking up towards the roof.

Chad sat on the roof. They'd decided on the second day, when Max was still in bed, that the roof gave the best vantage point. Mandy and James had rigged up a piece of twine that ran down from the roof to a bell inside the house. That way, whoever was on watch on the roof could pull on the twine and give a warning to anyone inside.

Chad was still huge, but he was already looking leaner. He got the same amount of food as everyone else. To his credit, he was toughening up considerably, now that he was sober. He rarely ever complained about the food or the portion sizes.

Chad gave Max the thumbs up sign. It wasn't like they could have an easy conversation from up on the high roof to down where Max was.

Max stood there, enjoying the sun, while trying to think about what they were going to do for water. Soon, he'd go inspect the well, but he didn't expect to find much there. If the well was drying up, he didn't know what they'd be able to do about it. Their best bet was to get water from a nearby creek, and then purify it if they could.

But the whole plan meant a lot of work, and it meant exposing themselves more to a potential attack. The creek was a good twenty minute walk. It meant potentially giving away their position to someone who happened to be walking by.

The sound of a bell reached Max through his veil of deep thoughts.

At first, Max thought maybe he was hearing things.

No, it was definitely the bell, the sound faint and muffled, coming from inside the farmhouse.

Max looked up to see Chad turned around, facing the

other direction. He faced towards the road, which was a good distance from the farmhouse. A long dirt driveway wound its way from the road to the farmhouse. While Max had been recovering in bed, the rest of them had done their best to disguise the driveway's entrance. They hoped that someone coming down the road wouldn't notice it, but merely drive right on by.

"What's going on?" said James. He still had sleep in his eyes as he came down the porch steps. Sadie followed him. "Is everyone all right?"

Max looked up at Chad, who turned to face him.

"Car," mouthed Chad, as clearly as he could.

"Looks like Chad's spotted a car," said Max.

"What do we do?" said James. There was worry in his voice.

"Where are your guns?" said Max, looking James and Sadie up and down. He spoke to them harshly. But there was a reason for his tone. They were supposed to carry their rifles with them everywhere, no matter what. Max had told them a thousand times that they were lucky their mother had had such a large quantity of guns. And those guns would likely save their lives one day. This wasn't the time for sloppiness.

"We were just coming out to see..." said Sadie, trying to make an excuse.

"We'll get them," said James, cutting off his sister.

Sadie's expression turned to embarrassment and shame. They both knew how important following the rules was.

"It's coming down the driveway," said Chad, turning over his shoulder to speak to Max.

So much for their efforts to conceal the driveway.

Max could hear the car now. He could hear its engine whining softly. It sounded like a regular civilian car. It didn't have that heavy rumbling of a large truck. That was a good sign, but it didn't mean they were safe.

Anyone could be driving that car.

This was the moment Max had been waiting for and dreading. The worst part about it was that he wasn't yet in fighting form. He was still hobbled, injured, and partially broken.

But that didn't mean he was going to give up.

He knew he could still put up a hell of a fight.

Max reached for his Glock in its belt holster. The weight of the gun felt reassuring as he removed it from its holster. He kept his finger outside the trigger guard. Just because society had collapsed didn't mean he wasn't going to follow basic gun safety. The last thing they needed was another gunshot victim.

"What do we do?" said Chad, making an effort to speak loudly enough that Max could hear him.

"Stay there," said Max.

Chad had his rifle with him, but he wasn't a great shot. He'd only fired a gun a few times in his life before. Despite Georgia's patient training, he still wasn't very good. And it wasn't like they could waste a lot of ammunition on practice shots.

Max started to hobble his way around the house.

Suddenly, James and Sadie were at his side again, this time with rifles in hand.

"What's going on?" said James.

"It's coming down the driveway," said Max.

All three of them could clearly hear the engine, clearly hear the tires on the partially-graveled driveway. But they couldn't yet see the car. The house was blocking the view.

"My mom's not back yet from her hunt?" said Sadie.

"I wish she was," said Max. "She's the best shot out of all of us."

It was true.

"What are we going to do?" said James, his voice full of worry.

Max was worried too. He felt the adrenaline pumping through him. He felt his skin growing cold and his heart rate increasing. But he had to keep it together. And he couldn't afford to let James and Sadie know that he was scared.

Being scared was only natural. He was only human, after all.

Max knew it was what you did with the fear that mattered. It was how you responded to it.

If he gave a hint to James or Sadie of his own fear, they'd just become more terrified. Max knew he needed them to be as effective as possible. It was likely that he wouldn't be able to do what he needed to do on his own.

And he couldn't rely on Chad up on the roof. If Georgia had been up there, acting essentially as a sharpshooter, he would have been a lot less worried.

They were halfway around the house. James and Sadie followed Max, who had to move somewhat slowly with his cane. Frankly, it was almost miraculous that he could walk at all, let alone go as fast as he was.

"What's that?" said Sadie, suddenly sounding even more worried than before.

"Shh," said James. "We have to listen."

"No, seriously," said Sadie. "Look over there."

From where they were, around the side of the house, they could see three figures emerging from the woods. If you could call where the car was approaching on the driveway the front yard, then the figures were coming from the backyard.

"Shit," muttered Max, staring at the figures.

They were far away, but he could see them clearly enough to note that they were armed. They had rifles. Possibly assault rifles.

Suddenly, Max remembered something. Someone was missing.

"Where's Mandy?" said Max.

"Mandy?" said James.

"Yeah, you didn't see her inside when you went to get your guns?"

"No," said Sadie. "I thought she was outside somewhere."

"Shit," muttered Max.

The sound of the car on the driveway was louder. It was getting very close.

They had two sets of unknown visitors. And Mandy was missing.

3

MANDY

Maybe Mandy was taking the whole thing harder than she should. After all, this was a crazy situation they were all in. They were lucky to be alive. Maybe expecting that something would have happened between her and Max was simply unrealistic. In fact, she knew it was unrealistic. Remaining "colleagues" or whatever they were was obviously the best choice. She knew that, but she was still feeling down about it.

When Max had gone to check on the well, Mandy had left through the door on the other side of the house. All six of the group had argued often over which door was the front and which was the back. They had arrived to the farmhouse initially from the side that faced the woods. Since that was their first impression, that side of the house had become "the front" for about half of them. But others argued that the side that faced the road was the front.

Mandy didn't really care either way.

She had her rifle with her as she walked through the

long grass and the weeds. She walked alongside the driveway that led towards the road. It was a winding path.

The sun was out, shining brightly. The grass swayed in the wind. But it didn't look beautiful to Mandy.

So much had changed. Her mind was having trouble adapting to her new situation. It was having trouble adapting to this new world.

To say that everything had changed would be an understatement.

As she walked, she thought of the people she knew. She thought of her parents, her brother, her aunts and uncles. She thought of the other waitresses at work, and even of her difficult boss. She thought of random classmates from high school and even middle school. What had happened to them all?

According to Max, almost everyone was dead or was in the process of dying.

Without any sort of communication, there was no way to know. There wasn't internet, TV, or phones. And it wasn't like the postal system was functioning.

Maybe some day in the future, Mandy would find her family alive, safely holed up somewhere.

But she tried not to get her hopes up. She knew better than that.

She'd learned a lot in the last two weeks. She'd learned what it was like to be hungry, to go without. She'd learned to deal with the desperation she felt like a heavy pit in her stomach.

Mandy was far from the house. She turned back to look at it. It looked peaceful there, surrounded by nature, by fields that led into the forest.

Chad lay on the roof. If it hadn't been for his rifle, he

would have perhaps looked like he was lounging, rather than defending the house's inhabitants from apocalyptic hordes.

Suddenly, Mandy heard a noise.

She was so surprised that she froze in place.

It was unmistakably the sound of a car traveling down the road.

So there were others. People were still alive, and some of them had functioning cars and even gas to burn on drives.

Maybe they were people like Georgia and the farmhouse group. Or maybe they were the savage killers Max was always warning them all about.

With any luck, the car would pass right by the driveway. With any luck, disguising the entrance would work.

But just in case, Mandy moved quickly over to a large tree. The trunk was huge, and she hid herself behind it. If the car did come down the driveway, she'd be out of sight.

Mandy sat with her knees towards her chest, her rifle pointed towards the sky, its butt resting in the ground.

She breathed deeply as she waited for the car to pass by the driveway.

But it didn't.

She was halfway between the road and the farmhouse. From where she was, she could hear someone getting out of the car and moving the branches aside. She heard the gate opening, squeaking on its rusty hinges.

The car started driving down the driveway. Every sound, from its engines to its tires, sent another chill down Mandy's spine. Her hands were shaking with fear.

The solid bulk of the rifle felt somewhat reassuring in her hands, and she gripped it tighter. Her right hand moved down to a plastic knife sheath attached to her belt with some twine. It was a Mora utility knife, cheap and practical. It was decidedly unpretentious with its plastic handle and non-threatening blade shape, but the steel, Mandy had been told, was good quality carbon steel. Whatever that meant. Mandy just knew that putting her hand around the handle gave her some comfort. Whatever that was worth.

4

GEORGIA

The men had passed Georgia without seeing her. Georgia had waited a couple minutes, making sure there weren't more following, and to give herself a wide enough berth.

She'd followed the three men through the forest. They were headed right towards the farmhouse, even changing their path, seemingly accidentally, to cut a more direct route.

Georgia crouched in the underbrush, not far from where the forest met the field. The men stood right at the boundary, speaking loudly.

"Looks like we're in luck," said one of them, speaking loudly.

"You think someone's in there?"

"Can you even see? There's someone up there on the roof."

"Up on the roof? Oh yeah, I see him. What's he doing up there?"

"You're even dumber today for some reason."

"Lay off me, man."

"I don't want to have to give you another beating. Do you want that?"

"No."

So there was contention among the "ranks" of these three men. Georgia filed that information away for later. It might be useful. And maybe sooner than she'd hoped for. Practically all she could think about was that she wished these men had never come along, never found the farmhouse.

Max had told her about his plans for rudimentary defense systems. He'd described a trench, maybe a fence. But everything was still in the planning stages, and the projects weren't even off the ground yet. It was almost impossible to think about spending days exhausting themselves digging a trench when there was hardly enough food to eat.

But that was the way surviving worked. You had to think clearly about your energy levels, even when you were exhausted. Calories meant something different now than before the EMP. Now, you didn't want to waste them on anything that wasn't crucial.

"OK, so I'll have to spell it out for you, I guess," the man was saying. "There are people in that house, and that man on the roof is up there to defend it. Or to keep watch. Or both. And what's worth defending is worth stealing, am I right?"

"Damn right."

"Hell yeah," said the other.

"All right, we'll move out soon."

These guys spoke in a way that made it seem as if they imagined that they were some military unit. But Georgia knew that they weren't. They simply didn't use the right slang or the right expressions.

Georgia weighed her options.

Now she knew for certain that these men were intent on robbing the farmhouse. And Georgia had no reason to believe that they wouldn't use all the force at their disposal. They had assault rifles, and could easily outgun the farmhouse inhabitants.

Sure, it was three against six. But Georgia had a realistic understanding of her companions, and her children's, abilities with a gun. Mandy, Chad, and Sadie had hardly ever handled a gun before. James was quite a bit better, but that alone wouldn't be enough. Max knew what he was doing with his Glock, but he was injured, and Georgia didn't know if she could count on him now if things got tough.

Georgia had one of the men's heads trained in the sights of her rifle. She could squeeze the trigger and kill him in an instant. But she doubted she'd be able to get off two more shots, especially if the other two men charged her.

No, that wasn't the way to go. Georgia needed to stay alive if she wanted to protect James and Sadie, not to mention the rest.

Georgia crawled forward a little more, inching across the ground on her belly like some animal. From her new vantage point, she moved her rifle so that she could see Chad on the roof of the farmhouse through her scope.

If Chad had only been a good shot, maybe between the two of them they'd be able to take out the three men before any damage was done.

But Chad was by far the worst shot of them all. Even Sadie was better, and improving rapidly each target practice.

The best thing to do, Georgia decided, was to wait for the men to approach the farmhouse. Chad was sure to notice them, ring the bell, and alert the others. Then,

Georgia could take at least one of the men out. That would give everyone else more of a chance.

She just hoped the plan worked.

"Come on, man," one of the men was saying. "Let's just go already."

Georgia was thinking the same thing. She was used to waiting in silence, motionless. After all, she'd hunted for years. But this was different. When she'd hunted for deer, no human lives were at stake. Especially not those of her only children. She could feel her anxiety building, a physical sensation in her body. Her chest felt tight, and her stomach was in knots.

"Yeah," said another. "Let's just do it already. I'm tired of waiting. What are you looking for anyway through those binoculars?"

"I'm trying to figure out how many people we're up against."

"What's the difference? We did fine on the last raids."

"We did fine on the last raids because I scouted everything out perfectly beforehand."

Two of the men sounded almost impossibly dumb to Georgia. Dumb, cruel people could be dangerous. But the leader sounded intelligent and cruel, which in her opinion was a much more dangerous combination.

"Well," said the leader. "I don't see anyone else. Maybe you two are right. Let's make a move on it."

"Finally."

"Get 'er going, that's what."

Georgia breathed a sigh of relief. Her plan was going to be difficult and dangerous, but at least she could finally get on with it.

All she needed was for Chad to spot them, which shouldn't be hard for him to do, considering how the men had stomped through the forest so loudly. Even if their leader was intelligent, they weren't the subtle types.

Georgia had been watching the men, but now she checked Chad again in her scope.

To her horror, Chad had turned around. He was facing the wrong way. She kept watching him for a few impossibly long seconds, hoping he'd turn around. But he didn't.

Shit.

If Chad didn't see them coming, and everyone else was inside, it would be a blood bath. The men could simply enter the house, and pepper everyone with bullets before they'd even reached their guns. And rifles certainly weren't the best weapons for a situation like that. Even worse, the men might be able to shoot through the exterior walls before entering.

Georgia didn't know what to do. And that was an understatement.

5

JOHN

John had been holed up in his Center City apartment for the last two weeks. Currently, he was crouched in a corner, back up against the wall, arms around his knees.

The apartment had been luxurious and inviting when the electricity was running. Now, it felt like a prison cell designed by the demented.

His thoughts were drifting. He was somewhere between being awake and being asleep.

He thought of his family. He wondered what'd happened to his brother, Max.

John and Max hadn't been close for the last decade. They'd simply drifted apart. Their family hadn't really been a "talking" family, so John figured that he and Max simply had trouble opening up and communicating with each other.

Max, as far as John knew, had been living out in the suburbs still. He'd been offered higher-paying jobs in the city, but he'd refused them all. At the time, John simply couldn't fathom why Max would want to stay out in the boring suburbs with his boring job.

Now, Max's decision made more sense.

Not that John knew Max had gotten out safely. In fact, there was absolutely no way to know. There were no phones, no internet, no means of communication whatsoever.

Max had always been talking about his plans for "when the shit hit the fan." Well, that was about ten years ago. John, and everyone else, had always scoffed at Max's prediction of a violent end to modern society. And as far as John had seen, Max hadn't actually taken any steps to do anything about what he'd feared. Maybe, though, sometime in the last decade, Max had gotten more into it. Who knew. John now wished he'd talked to Max more. He wished he'd done a lot of things differently, and spent his time with different people. John had wasted so many hours of his life hobnobbing in the fancy Center City bars with the other investor types, always hoping for a hot tip or a new business contact.

The entire apartment was dark, except for thin rays of light that broke through the expensive blinds and curtains he'd purchased last year.

He'd heard screams almost every day. He'd heard moaning and crying coming from the other apartments. He'd heard the unmistakable sound of a gunshot in the hallway.

Once, someone had banged loudly on his door. He hadn't answered it, of course, and eventually the person had gone away. But John had spent that entire half hour in complete panic, his fist gripping a large kitchen knife.

John had run out of food four days ago. Up until then, he'd been eating uncooked and partially rotten food from his freezer. A year ago, he'd purchased half of a cow through one of those organic farm share type programs. He'd never gotten around to eating anything but the finest steaks, so what had remained after the EMP were mostly organ meats that had once seemed completely unappetizing. Not that they had suddenly become delicacies, but John had sucked down a half-rotten raw kidney greedily. That was what hunger did to you.

Since the EMP, John had been drinking water out of his tub. He was now approaching the bottom of the tub, and it was difficult to gather the water into the coffee mug he used as a ladle. He didn't know if he could drink the tap water or not.

John wasn't stupid. He hadn't left his apartment since the EMP. He'd known something was up, and as he'd walked home from work that day, he'd recognized the signs of an EMP.

Initially, John hadn't considered leaving the city. After all, he'd been sure that the government would leap into action. He'd been sure that the power would be back on in a few days. But the days had ticked by, and now two weeks had passed without a single flicker of the lights. John had to admit now that he'd been wrong, and now he no longer held even a shred of hope that things would return to normal.

At least John had had enough sense to stay holed up in his apartment. He'd known there'd be chaos during the power outage, but he'd been sure that law and order would be restored.

He was shaking as he crouched there. His coffee mug was on the floor next to him. There was also the large kitchen knife, and a couple other odds and ends. The apartment was a mess, filled with the smelly plastic the frozen meat had come in. The freezer and fridge themselves stank horribly as well. But John hardly noticed that now.

There was a blood-curdling scream that came from the hallway of the apartment building.

John froze in fear.

Everything was more terrifying in the near-darkness.

He couldn't imagine what it was like in those hallways, now pitch-black. John was on the fifth level, and he knew the stairways leading down would be nothing but terrifying darkness.

The scream continued for a full minute.

There were other sounds. A strange thumping sound. The sound of something banging into the wall. Then the unmistakable sound of a fist against a skull.

John had to get out of here.

He'd been denying it for as long as he could.

But there was no food left. He'd die soon enough if he stayed there.

The screaming stopped suddenly. It was nothing but piercing silence now.

John's heart was thumping wildly. He was sure he wasn't thinking clearly. The only thought that echoed through his rattled mind was: get out.

He didn't care if he wasn't making the right decision. As far as he was concerned, it was the only decision.

John's mind turned again to his estranged brother, Max. If Max had done what he'd been threatening to do and finally gotten prepared, there'd be one place that Max would have fled to. And that was the farmhouse that he'd inherited.

John was still bitter about the farmhouse. It was one of those familial disagreements that outsiders could never understand. John made a hell of a lot of money, and it wasn't as if the farmhouse had any financial value for him. Instead, it was that he had been passed over, simply because Max had gotten along better with their grandfather.

John got up suddenly. It was time to act.

It was time to leave.

He didn't think he could really make it to the farmhouse. He didn't even really think that Max would be there. After all, Max was probably dead. And John probably wouldn't make it.

Moving frantically in the dim light, John gathered what he could. There was no food to take with him. Really, there was hardly anything that might be useful. His luxurious apartment had been outfitted in the minimalist style of expensive pieces of furniture. The style left no room for odds and ends to lay around. And John wasn't the type to keep tools or camping gear around.

In the span of five minutes, John gathered his things.

In one hand, he held his kitchen knife. He gripped it so tightly his knuckles were almost white.

In his other hand, he held his expensive leather briefcase. Inside, he had stuffed a flannel-lined raincoat. It was perhaps the most practical piece of clothing that he owned. The briefcase also contained a water bottle John had discovered at the last minute in one of the mostly-unused kitchen cupboards.

There was no flashlight to be found in the apartment. He didn't have any candles either. He was going to have to do this in the dark.

The light outside was dimming. The sun was going down.

It was now or never.

John knew he'd rather die outside than spend another

moment starving to death in his apartment. He had to at least try. He had that much life left in him.

But he wasn't sure he'd even make it through the hallway alive.

Knife in hand, he swung the front door open.

The hallway was dark. But with the doorway open, some of the sun's dying light came through the blinds in a line across the hallway.

A woman's body lay on the floor. Her hair was matted with blood.

John looked away immediately. He didn't want to see her injuries.

He stepped over her body.

The sunlight got dimmer the farther he walked.

His heart had never beat harder or faster.

He was almost paralyzed with fear.

But he kept going.

He wasn't going to give up. He'd finally found the strength to leave. He was finally willing to fight. He was finally willing to try to survive.

It was the trying that was important.

After all, he didn't expect to live.

At the end of the hallway, the light was so dim he almost couldn't see.

He'd passed by the elevator. Obviously that wasn't an option.

John stood in front of the heavy metal door that led to the stairwell, normally only used in emergencies. Well, this is an emergency, he thought.

He took a deep breath. Holding his knife in front of him, ready to stab, he pushed the door open.

Not that he'd be able to see a potential attacker.

He stepped across the threshold and the heavy metal door slammed closed behind him.

John couldn't see his hand in front of him. He had no idea where the stairs began. He'd have to crawl on his hands and knees.

The farmhouse was at least an eight hours' drive from the city. And John hadn't even left his building yet. And he was currently crawling.

6

MAX

They had to deal with the approaching car first. It was closer than the figures across the field.

"What do we do?" whispered James.

"We wait to see who they are and what they want," said Max.

Max certainly wasn't above killing someone who was a threat. But at the same time, he wasn't simply going to shoot someone for driving onto his property.

Hidden behind the corner of the house, they'd watched the minivan drive up the long driveway.

Maybe the fact that it was a minivan factored into his thinking. But Max knew that wasn't rational. While a minivan conveyed the idea of an innocent family, anyone could be driving it. It wasn't like owning a minivan made someone not dangerous, not a threat.

The minivan sat there. The driver turned the engine off. But Max couldn't see the driver because of the glare on the windows.

Finally, after what seemed like forever, the driver's side door opened.

A man stepped out. Max couldn't see him at first. The driver's side door was on the opposite side from where Max was, and the body of the van blocked his view.

"Anyone there?" shouted the van's driver.

The driver walked in front of the van.

He was tall and lanky, wearing a dress shirt that was partially torn along the side. He had about two weeks' growth of beard, and his hair was disheveled and long. He looked like he might be of college age.

Max gave James and Sadie a sign not to move, by putting his finger to his lips. Then he gave them a sign to stay where they were.

Max moved slowly away from where James and Sadie were. His leg was killing him, but he pushed himself. He didn't want to be by James and Sadie, in case there was any danger. He figured it was better to have his backup in a different position, anyway.

The van driver didn't appear to be armed. But Max knew you couldn't trust appearances.

"What do you want?" said Max loudly, giving away his position.

The man turned to look at him. His face broke into an expression of relief. He started walking towards Max.

Max planted his feet and pointed his Glock at the man. "Stay right there," he said, speaking loudly and clearly. "Put your hands in the air."

"Hey, I'm not here to hurt anyone... I'm just looking for..."

"Shut up," said Max. "Stay where you are, or I shoot. Do you have any weapons?"

"Nope," said the man. "I'm just looking for a place to stay... I was driving across the country and then something happened..."

Was it possible that this college-aged guy didn't understand what had happened?

Max didn't trust this guy, as a matter of pure precaution and common sense.

But he recognized that he might have information about the rest of the country.

When Max asked the question, he knew in the pit of his stomach that he already knew the answer.

"Is the power out everywhere?" said Max.

"Across the whole country."

Max wondered how the man had gotten across the whole country without running out of gas, and without getting killed in the process. Maybe he'd been lucky. Or maybe he was lying.

Suddenly, a shot rang out from the other side of the house.

"What the hell?" shouted the man, startled.

There was yelling coming from the other side of the house. And the voices didn't sound like anyone who lived at the farmhouse. It was those figures they'd seen.

Max's heart was pounding. His body filled with adrenaline.

He wished he knew where Mandy was.

"Get farther back, and keep your rifles out," he shouted towards James and Sadie. He needed them to get away from the house. If whoever was on the other side came around that side of the house, James and Sadie would be directly in their path. He needed them farther away for their safety, and for their rifles to be any good in a fight.

Max didn't have much time. But he hobbled forward another couple steps. He raised his Glock to point directly at the man's head.

"Did you plan this?" he shouted at the man.

"No! I don't know what the hell's going on. I swear..."

Max saw the terror in his face, and he believed him. Not that it did him much good.

Suddenly, Max saw two men racing around the far side of the house. They rounded the corner, assault rifles in their hands. Everything was happening too fast. Max could barely take everything in. But he saw their ruthlessness in the way they moved.

One crouched, using the corner of the house as a partial shield. He lowered his gun and let forth several shots.

The minivan driver crumpled to the ground. He'd been hit in the stomach.

It was all happening too fast.

But Max threw himself to the ground, his arms stretched in front of himself. He returned fire with his Glock. But the distance was too great. He missed, his bullets hitting the house instead of the assailant.

Another shot rang out. It must have been James or Sadie. Probably James.

It missed, hitting the ground, sending a clump of dirt flying into the air.

The men with the assault rifles retreated behind the side of the house, out of view.

"Chad!" shouted Max.

Why wasn't Chad shooting them?

Maybe because he was terrified, hiding in the middle of the roof. From where he lay, Max couldn't even see Chad now. Not that it mattered much. Chad was a terrible shot, and they all knew it, including Chad himself.

With the men out of sight, Max took his chance. He scrambled to his feet the best he could. His leg was killing him. But he managed to retreat backwards. He kept his Glock trained on where the men had been.

Finally, after what felt like an eternity, he made it to some bushes.

"James," he hissed.

"Right over here," came James's reply.

"What's going on?" said Sadie, her voice low. Max could hear the terror in her voice.

Max didn't answer.

"Just stay alert," he said.

He felt like he needed to give the kids some guidance, give them some instructions.

But the truth was that Max himself was way out of his element. Sure, he'd had plenty of practice at the firing range. And now he actually had to shoot people, rather than just basic targets. Max recognized that he simply didn't know much about strategy in a situation like this. The best he could do was rely on his instincts.

Relying on his instincts was hard with his leg. The pain was coursing through him. He wasn't supposed to be moving his leg this much.

James and Sadie crawled over to where Max was. They were right next to him.

"What's happening?" said James. "Do you know who fired that shot?"

Max shook his head.

The minutes ticked by. The waiting felt like an eternity. There wasn't another sign of the armed attackers.

Max glanced at the corpse of the college-aged man lying in front of the house. There wasn't a breath of life in him. His eyes were wide open. The front of his shirt was soaked with blood.

The minivan still sat there, the driver's door wide open.

It was as if the minivan with its open door was inviting them. It was the perfect escape. With a little luck, they could make it into the van without getting shot. They could drive away from here.

But they couldn't do that.

They couldn't leave Chad on the roof.

And they couldn't leave behind Mandy and Georgia.

On the roof of the house, Max finally saw Chad reappear.

Max waved at him, trying to get his attention. But Chad didn't seem to see him.

"Psst," came a voice from off to the side.

"Mom?" said Sadie.

Max turned. It was Georgia, her hunting clothes drenched in sweat. Her hair was wet and plastered down, stuck to her forehead. It looked like she'd been running hard.

"Where'd you come from?" said James. "Are you OK?"

Georgia was breathing so heavily it seemed hard for her to talk. She came over to where the three of them lay behind the cover of the bushes and tree trunks.

She got down with them, setting her rifle in front of her. She had her priorities straight, and didn't speak until she got her rifle in position.

"I shot one of them," she said, her voice breathless. "There were three. Two left."

"We saw them," said Max. "They shot him."

"Who?"

Max gestured to the corpse on the ground by the van.

"Who the hell is he?"

"We don't know," said Max. "He just showed up."

"Shit."

"You shot one of them, Mom?" said Sadie, her voice full of terror.

"I had to," said Georgia. "I overheard them. I don't know

who they are exactly. But what I know is that they've been traveling around, taking what they need and what they want. They've been killing indiscriminately, from the sound of it. I heard them talking about killing us all and taking the house. Or what's in the house."

"This is what I was afraid of," muttered Max.

"Well, you'll be happy to know you were right."

"Doesn't make me happy."

"They're heavily armed," said Georgia. "One had an AR-15."

"Shit."

"What's an AR-15?" said Sadie.

"Assault rifle," said James. He sounded worried, but he was keeping it together. Max was impressed. Not that he had much time to think about that now.

Max knew they needed a plan.

"Where are they now?" said Max.

"I don't know. After I shot the one, the two others just kept running. They were almost at the house. I came around the long way on the side."

"Why didn't Chad do anything?"

"I don't know. Maybe he froze up," said Georgia.

"Damn it," muttered Max. "Any ideas on what to do, Georgia?"

It had been almost fifteen minutes now. And there wasn't a single sign or sound from the armed men.

"Maybe they've left," said Sadie.

"I doubt it," said Max. "You said they were definitely coming for the farmhouse, right, Georgia?"

"Yeah," said Georgia. "They sounded vicious and cruel. There was something horrible about their voices, and the way they talked."

"Sounds like they're the kind of men who'll do anything

to get what they want," said Max. "I doubt they're simply going to leave because I fired a couple shots at them."

Max looked up at Chad on the roof.

This time, Chad was looking at him.

Chad was making gestures with his hands and his arms. But it didn't look like any kind of system of symbols that Max could recognize.

"Any idea what he's trying to say?"

"No idea," said Georgia.

Now Chad was pointing directly down at the house. He kept pointing down, using both hands, occasionally moving his arms for added emphasis.

"I think he's saying the men are in the house," said James.

"Shit, I think you might be right," said Max.

"What's going to happen?" said Sadie.

"It's going to be OK, Sadie," said Georgia. "Let's try to figure this out."

"Mandy was out of the house, right?" said Max.

"She definitely wasn't in there," said James.

"Definitely not," said Sadie. "We would have seen her."

"The only problem is we don't know where she is."

"What are you thinking?" said Georgia.

Max had his eyes on the house. Suddenly, there was a flash of movement in one of the upstairs windows. One of the men appeared in the window, his torso visible. But it was too quick for anyone to get a shot. He disappeared from view a second later.

"They're definitely in the farmhouse," said Max. "And there's no way we're going to be able to enter it and take it back with force. Not with a bunch of rifles. And I'm not good for anything quick, not with this leg."

Max may not have been a brilliant military strategist, but

he had a realistic understanding of the situation. In the movies, the hero would simply storm the house and shoot the bad guys dead, all without getting injured. But Max knew that he didn't have those abilities, that those sorts of things were generally fiction.

Plus, with his injured leg, there was no chance of doing that.

"I think the best thing to do," said Max, "is to let them stay in there."

"All our stuff's in there!" said Sadie.

"Shut up," said James.

"She's got a good point," said Max. "We need our stuff to survive. And we probably need the house, too. I'm not saying we're going to let them take it."

"You're thinking of staying out on the fringes and picking them off when they finally have to come out?" said Georgia.

"Exactly," said Max. "There's hardly any food in there. They're going to have to come out at some point."

"They were wearing big packs," said Georgia. "And it sounded like they'd robbed a lot of people... I'm sure they'll have food with them."

"Well," said Max. "We're going to have to wait if we want to get the house back. The only other option is to leave."

"Leave?" said James.

"We could take the minivan," said Max. "But we'd be starting all over. And without most of our gear. I think that's going to have to be option number two."

"What about Chad?" said Sadie. "He's stuck up there on the roof."

"He's going to have to just wait it out," said Max. "And hopefully we'll see Mandy before she tries to enter the house."

"This would be a lot easier if our cell phones worked," said Sadie.

"Shut up," said James. "You're not helping."

There were times when their sibling rivalry could be cute, but this wasn't one of them. It was starting to wear on Max.

"Kids," said Georgia. "Come on now."

"Yeah, James," said Sadie.

"She's got a good point," said Max. "But there's nothing we can do about that."

"What if they try to leave in the van?" said Georgia. "We're going to have to cover both doors... They could easily rush out the front, and get into the van with a bunch of our supplies."

"Yeah," said Max. "What's stopping them from simply gathering up the best of our possessions and leaving."

"I don't think so," said Georgia. "I have a feeling they're going to want the house. They were... it's hard to describe their attitude. But they just want to take. They want complete control..."

On the roof, Chad was still pointing down into the house, indicating that he hadn't seen the men leave yet.

"Either way," said Max. "We'll shoot them when they leave. They're probably more likely to leave the way they came in. You're the best shot by far, Georgia. So you're going to need to move out. You know what to do. Find good cover, and wait. There aren't going to be any shifts. We're going to have to stay awake as long as possible. Here, these might be useful."

Max took a bottle of strong caffeine pills from his pocket. He shook some into Georgia's hand. "You're going to want to take them frequently."

"What are you going to do?"

"Stay here," said Max. "James will stay with me. Sadie should go with you. James is a better shot than Sadie, and I need him here. I might not be much good with this leg, and I only have my Glock."

"Makes sense," said Georgia. "We'd better head out now."

"If you see Mandy," said Max. "Do everything you can to warn her. Fire a shot in the air if you have to. She might be too far to reach by shouting."

"Got it, come on, Sadie... And be careful, James."

There was the hint of a tear in her eye as she crawled over to James and gave him a half hug, which looked hard to do because they were all flat on their stomachs on the ground.

"Take care of Sadie, Mom," said James.

Sadie looked terrified, but she followed her mom.

Georgia knew what to do. Max wasn't too worried about them. Keeping his eyes on the house, he watched out of his peripheral vision as Georgia and Sadie crawled away. They'd take the long away around the house, keeping out of sight as much as possible.

Everything was falling apart. Max liked to run a tight ship. And the situation right now was anything but. They'd lost their house, and their gear.

"OK," whispered Max to James, who moved until he was right next to Max. "I didn't want to worry them, but we're going to need to get that van out of there."

"The van?" said James. "Why?"

"We might need it for ourselves. It's too valuable to let them get away with it, not to mention all our gear."

Max's eyes traveled again to the college-aged man dead on the ground, his eyes still wide open.

7

MANDY

Mandy had thought she'd toughened up over the last two weeks. She'd seen bodies. She'd seen people shot. To say she'd been OK with it all would be completely wrong. But she was getting used to it, adapting as people do to intense new circumstances.

But all that adaptation was failing her now.

She was still behind the tree, out of view.

Her whole body was shaking with fear. She felt sick to her stomach, like she might vomit at any moment.

The adrenaline was coursing through her. Her vision had narrowed down to a tight tunnel.

She held the gun, but her hands were shaking so much, she doubted she'd be able to use it.

She'd felt like this before, years before, when applying for her waitressing job. She'd felt like she was going to pass out, just sitting in her car, application in hand. Later, a friend had told her it had sounded like a panic attack.

If that was a panic attack, then what she was experiencing now was certainly a panic attack.

What timing.

She needed to be moving. She needed to take action.

But instead she was frozen.

Maybe it was the weeks of dwindling food supplies. Maybe it was the constant stress. Maybe it had all built up to this.

Mandy had hidden behind the tree as the van drove up the road. She'd heard voices in the distance, towards the house. Then she'd heard the unmistakable sound of gunfire.

Now all was quiet. And Mandy waited. She didn't know what'd happened. She was too terrified to look. She was horrified at the thought that Max or Georgia or any of the others had been shot.

She didn't know who had done the shooting. She didn't know who was in the van.

The sun was low in the sky. Within an hour, it would be nightfall.

Mandy knew that tonight the moon would be bright. Not that that gave her much comfort.

Should she head towards the house? She knew she was playing the coward. Maybe her friends desperately needed her help.

She couldn't just sit there, waiting. She didn't know how much time had passed. She didn't have a watch. She'd always checked the time on her cell phone. But that was before the EMP. Before everything had changed.

Finally, Mandy forced herself to her feet. It took all her willpower. She peeked out from behind the thick tree trunk.

The house still stood. There was no movement anywhere. She couldn't see if Chad was on the roof or not. The van was there. From where she was, it looked as if the doors were all closed. She couldn't see over to the other side, however.

Where was everyone?

Mandy's eyes scanned the area, looking for something, some sign of what had happened.

That was when she saw the body lying on the ground. Whoever it was, they were clearly dead. But Mandy wasn't close enough to see properly.

She remembered the scope on her hunting rifle. She felt like an idiot for not thinking of it before. Then again, she still wasn't used to carrying a gun.

Her hands shaking, Mandy pointed the rifle at the body. Using the scope, she could see that it was a man. She breathed a sigh of relief when she saw that it wasn't one of her friends. Maybe he was the man who'd driven the van.

Maybe he'd attacked the farmhouse group, and been killed. Maybe it was safe now to go back into the farmhouse.

But Mandy hesitated. She didn't know why, except that it was strange there wasn't any movement around the house. Normally, someone would have come out to do something. Wasn't Max going to check that well? And why wasn't Chad on the roof?

It was possible, of course, that he was merely on the other side. But the rules of the watch that Max had laid out clearly stated that the watchman needed to keep an eye out in all directions.

Mandy heard a sound behind her.

It sounded like someone walking through the long grass, a soft, swishing sound. It was so soft Mandy wasn't sure if she was really hearing it or not. Maybe she was imagining things in her heightened state of awareness and fear.

Mandy spun around.

A stranger was walking towards her. It was a woman, only about five feet from Mandy.

The woman had long brown hair that was matted. Her

eyes shone with something, some intense look that chilled Mandy to the bone.

The woman didn't speak. She stood still, looking at Mandy, eying her, eying her rifle.

"Hello?" said Mandy.

The woman didn't answer.

She was practically skin and bones, already quite gaunt. Mandy's fear shot up another level. Mandy saw that the woman was desperate. Maybe she'd been a normal person before the EMP. Now she was a shell of her former self, hungry and desperate. She looked like she'd do anything.

The silence hung heavy between them. The moment seemed to stretch forever.

A thought shot through Mandy's brain—how strange that two strangers had shown up the same day.

Then again, maybe Max was right. He'd predicted that around this time survivors would reach these parts. And he'd predicted that they'd be desperate, ready to do anything. Max had said these people would have absolutely nothing to lose. And that they'd already lost their humanity.

The woman in front of Mandy suddenly rushed forward, charging Mandy.

Mandy acted instinctually. She swung her rifle at the woman. The butt of the gun collided with the woman's side. It made a sickening sound.

Mandy didn't want to hurt anyone. She never had. But her instincts were kicking in. It was either Mandy or the stranger.

And Mandy wasn't going to give herself up.

She'd do what she had to do, however horrible.

The woman grunted in pain.

But it wasn't enough to stop her.

Before the EMP, Mandy had never been in a fight before in her life. She'd gone to a school where only the boys fought, and even then only rarely.

The stranger grabbed the rifle, and she held on tight. Moving her leg, she shot her knee up. It connected with Mandy's groin, sending pain shooting through her. The pain was almost too much for her.

They were locked in a battle for the rifle. Both of them held it. It swayed this way and that, like two arms locked in an arm wrestling match. Neither would give up. Their eyes were locked.

A silence hung in the air. Neither of them spoke a word. Mandy heard only her own breathing, as well as the stranger's.

The stranger, despite being starving, had an incredible strength to her. It was strength that frightened Mandy.

Mandy remembered the knife in its plastic sheath. It might be her only hope. If she lost control of the rifle, she would certainly be shot.

Killing Mandy would only give the stranger the belongings she had on her. And she didn't have any food with her. But it wasn't about logic. It was about the instinct for survival, an instinct that could drive nearly anyone to do things they'd normally shudder to think about. It was an instinct that could cause horrible violence and pain, and not even necessarily for any reason, except that the instincts had become too strong...

Mandy could already feel her arms getting weak. Their legs were somehow locked together, as Mandy held the stranger's knee between her thighs, which she pressed tightly together.

It was a stalemate.

And there was only way out.

Mandy knew what she had to do. But she needed one hand free. That meant letting go of the gun. It was a dangerous plan. But it was the only one she had.

Mandy let go of the rifle with her right hand.

Doing so swung the balance of power towards the stranger. The stranger almost had the rifle now. Mandy couldn't hang onto it long with just one hand.

Her right hand found the plastic handle of the knife with the four-inch blade. It came out of the sheath easily.

Mandy didn't waste any time. She drove the knife forward with all her strength. It penetrated the woman's abdomen.

The stranger screamed. But she still clung to the rifle.

Mandy pulled the knife out, and stabbed again.

And again, and again.

Finally, the stranger collapsed to the ground. Blood covered her already stained and dirty shirt.

But the stranger wasn't dead.

Mandy acted quickly, while she knew she still had it in her. She didn't want the stranger to suffer more than she had to.

Mandy bent down and with a single motion, slit the woman's throat.

Mandy grabbed the rifle with one hand. Her knife, covered with blood, was in the other.

Mandy turned around, walked about four feet, and then bent over and vomited the little food she had in her stomach.

The world was a blur to Mandy. Without thinking, she moved automatically. With blood on her, she started trudging towards the farmhouse. She was in shock, horrified with what she'd done, and wasn't thinking about the gunshots she'd heard earlier.

The sun in the sky was setting, but Mandy didn't even notice.

8

JOHN

Somehow, John had made it down four flights of stairs. He figured he was at the ground floor now. He'd done it on his butt, with his hand on the guardrail, moving blindly. The entire time, he could only hope that there wasn't anyone in there with him. The screams he'd heard over the last two weeks were still fresh in his mind.

His briefcase was now slung over one shoulder, and the thin leather strap dug painfully into him. His kitchen knife was in his free hand.

He was still in the pitch-black darkness, but within minutes he'd found a door.

His hands gripped the solid steel metal bar of the door and he pushed.

Light came bursting in, shocking his darkness-adapted eyes.

John looked outside cautiously, sticking only his head out.

Shit, he'd found the wrong door. Maybe he'd lost count as he made his way down the flights of stairs. The truth was that John couldn't remember the last time he'd taken the stairs, if he ever had at all. He was an elevator man, as were most of the building's upscale occupants.

Well, it was the wrong door. But it was a door.

John shuddered at the thought of heading back into the darkness.

He stepped out the door and found himself behind the building in an alley.

John was already exhausted from the trip down the stairs. Maybe it was because of the hunger he felt like a pit in his stomach. Or maybe it was because he'd never worked out those muscles before. Not that he worked out much at all. His brother, Max, had always been the physically fit one, while John was more content to save his energy for his investment schemes.

Despite his fatigue, John started off down the alley. So far, everything looked normal.

Rounding the alley's exit, John found himself on Broad Street, which some called the pulse of Center City Philadelphia.

His jaw dropped as he gazed down the once-bustling city street.

Then again, he probably shouldn't have been surprised.

There were cars parked everywhere, abandoned, some with their doors open, as if people had fled quickly. Most of the cars were in the lanes, but some had been driven up onto the sidewalks before being abandoned.

The entire street was packed full of cars. There must have been a huge traffic jam to get out of the city. By the looks of it, most people had been stuck and never gotten out.

There wasn't a human in sight.

The street was desolate.

Except for a dog barking somewhere in the distance, there wasn't a single sound.

This wasn't what John had expected to find. He'd heard the noises, the screams. He'd heard it all. It had sounded like a complete madhouse, complete violent chaos. It had sounded like humanity turned completely savage and ruthless.

Maybe the flame of violence had burned bright, and then burned itself out. Maybe people had taken shelter in apartments and business buildings, waiting to starve together, too terrified to leave.

John didn't know what to do, so he started walking.

He walked along the sidewalk slowly. His mind was a tumbling mess of stupefaction. He was too hungry and shocked to have many thoughts.

The shop windows he passed were shattered. There was nothing inside the shops, when he looked.

It turned out John's first impression, that there were no people here, was wrong.

He saw his first body on the sidewalk. It was a young man, with his skull caved in. A bloody brick lay nearby.

John had no reaction. He was already too numb. He just stepped over the body and continued walking.

John headed west, towards the Schuylkill River that ran through the city.

In the first fifteen minutes, he saw many more bodies. He looked at them all. Afterwards, he didn't give them so much as a glance. Gradually, he stopped even noticing them. Call it shell shock or numbness, but John certainly wasn't himself. He'd been changed, perhaps permanently.

John wasn't even paying attention to where he was. He knew that he was walking west, and that was all that he cared about.

"Whoa, whoa, what the hell are you doing out here?"

The voice came out of nowhere.

John felt so out of it, so numb, that he didn't even look to see where the voice was coming from. His brain only half registered the sound.

The kitchen knife was still in his hand, but he had no intention of using it, even if the voice came from a threat.

"Hey there," said the voice again.

It came from a man, who scurried to catch up to John.

The man wore khaki pants and a button-down striped shirt. His hair was disarranged, and his once-respectable clothes were torn in various places.

"Hey, I'm talking to you. Can you hear me?"

Finally, John looked at the man. But he didn't stop walking.

"What do you want?" said John.

"I just want to help you," said the man. "I'm Lawrence J. Hekels. I was a social worker, a therapist, before this all started... all this chaos... I figure I'm still alive for a reason. And that reason is that I might just be able to help someone... What are you doing out walking around?"

"Got to get out," muttered John.

Lawrence Hekels walked alongside John.

The countless dead bodies had numbed John intensely. Maybe it was just too horrible for his brain to really comprehend. So it had started to shut down. But here was another human, alive. He was named Lawrence and he was speaking to John. This seemed to start waking John up a little.

John picked up his pace, walking faster, and Lawrence increased his own to keep up with him.

"I see you've got a knife there, but trust me, that's not going to be enough. We've got to get inside before the sun goes down."

"Why?" said John. "I'm getting out of the city. I don't want to starve to death."

"Trust me," said Lawrence. "I should be dead. I've spent too much time out on these streets. I've seen stuff you wouldn't imagine. Or maybe you can. I don't know what you've been through. The military has fallen. The police have fallen. It's just vicious gangs now. Really more of just a huge mob. And they mostly come out at night..."

John shrugged. "I don't really care," he said. "If I can get out first before I die... then that's fine with me..."

Lawrence spoke like a trained therapist. He spoke in easy-to-understand phrases. He kept his tone calm and level despite the situation.

"You say you don't want to starve," he said. "But trust me when I tell you it could be worse... Much worse..."

"What is this?" said John. "You're like an out-of-work therapist now or something? How are you going to help people at all with just mere words? I don't need words. I need weapons, or food, or water. Hell, I shouldn't even be talking to you. I should have just stabbed you when you came up to me. Now you don't seem like much of a threat. I can't believe you've lasted this long."

"I can't either," said Lawrence. "The truth is, I don't know what the hell I'm doing. I'm going to die soon anyway. I figured... Well, I might as well do as much good as I can now. And I don't have anything to offer except my words and advice. My whole life, I've tried to help people. I've taken the worst jobs in the worst areas... I've... Wait, did you hear that?"

"Hear what?" said John, stopping in his tracks. Despite what he said, he'd heard it too.

It was a deep rumbling off in the distance. It sounded like chanting, deep and ritualistic and terrifying.

"They're coming," said Lawrence. "Come on, we've got to get inside."

"What?" said John. "They don't go inside or something?"

"Oh," said Lawrence. "Of course they do, but if we're inside, at least we've got a chance of surviving. I've been lucky so far."

It was remarkable that Lawrence somehow spoke in his calm, professional tone, despite the situation.

John didn't know why, but something had changed within him. He didn't want to admit it to himself, but he knew that he wanted to survive. He knew that it was an impossible goal.

But maybe it'd be better to at least try for it...

He'd already decided to leave his apartment. He'd known that it'd be better to die trying to get out of the city, than waiting to starve to death.

But now he *really* wanted to try.

Despite his intense hunger, despite his thirst, despite his weakness, he was going to do everything he could.

"Come on," he said, jumping into action. He grabbed Lawrence's hand. "I know a place we can go."

"We've got to get into a building," said Lawrence.

"I know of one," said John. "Come with me."

The chanting was louder now. It sounded like a hundred voices mixed together. It almost didn't sound human. But as John was learning, humans could be more animalistic and intensely cruel than he'd ever imagined. Especially when driven to extreme ends, in extreme circumstances.

9

MAX

"Why don't we just shoot out the tires?" said James. "Or just one. That way, they wouldn't be able to use the van."

"You can drive on a flat tire," said Max. "Plus, I don't want to damage the van in any way. If what I think is happening is happening, we might need that van. And we might need to travel long distances in it."

"What do you think is happening?"

"I think my fears were right," said Max. "We made it out before most. Now the rest are following. More and more are going to be reaching this area. People are going to want to head in this direction, thinking they're escaping the worst of the worst in the cities and suburbs. They're bound to stumble on the farmhouse."

"So you think we're going to have to leave?" said James. "Where would we go?"

"No idea," said Max. "Let's focus on the plan right now."

"You think Chad is going to be OK up there?" said James. "What if they shoot up through the roof?"

"I hope they don't," said Max. "I don't know what we can do about it, though."

Max and James settled into silently watching the house. Max imagined that James was worried about his mother and his sister, but he didn't have any words of comfort for the kid. After all, the whole world was dangerous now, and it wasn't going to get any better.

"Hey," said James suddenly. "Look, it's Mandy."

Max turned his head.

Sure enough, it was Mandy, walking towards the house. She seemed to be walking strangely. In her right hand, she held a knife.

"Shit," muttered Max. "What the hell is she doing?"

"She doesn't know..." said James, apparently starting to state the obvious, and then realizing the futility of it.

"We've got to stop her," said Max.

Max was wondering if he should risk firing a shot in the air. But he didn't want the guys in the house to know that they were still out here.

"I'm going to go get her," said Max.

"No," said James. "I'll go."

"You're just a kid," said Max. "And you're likely to get killed."

"You'll never make it with that leg," said James.

Before Max could stop him, James was gone, leaving his rifle behind for Max.

Max took the rifle, putting his Glock back in its holster.

"Shit," muttered Max.

He didn't want to call out to James. That would give away their presence and position. Plus, he knew it wouldn't change James's mind.

James had impressed Max on more than a few occasions since moving into the farmhouse. He was growing up fast, maybe faster than he should have. But he was quickly becoming not only a man of his word, but a man who wanted to do the right thing, even when it was difficult.

But that didn't mean Max wanted James to risk his life right now.

Max watched as James moved swiftly, crouching low to the ground. He was headed right towards Mandy, who didn't seem to see him.

As Mandy got closer, Max realized she was in some kind of daze. Something had happened to her, and he felt a pang of regret in his stomach. He didn't know exactly where the regret was coming from, and he decided not to think about it, pushing it out of his mind.

Max couldn't keep watching, knowing that he had to keep his attention focused on the front door of the farmhouse. He wondered how Georgia and Sadie were doing, and he wondered about Chad, stuck up on that roof.

There was still no sign of movement inside the house.

The night was coming swiftly now, and Max wondered if this plan was really the best one, and whether it actually made any sense at all. It was hard to think clearly with the pain in his leg. And it was hard to think while so hungry. He just hoped they were doing the right thing.

Maybe it'd be better simply to get into the van and go, avoiding any possibility of armed conflict with the unknown men. Of course, they'd probably get shot in the process of trying to get into the van.

And of course it meant leaving Chad stranded on the roof. There didn't seem to be any way to rescue him.

Max simply couldn't leave Chad.

Maybe it was a weakness. Maybe it was a character flaw.

His companions might have said it was Max's greatest strength, the way he was always trying to look out for everyone. But right now, Max wasn't so sure. He feared the time when he'd allow his loyalty to his companions to seriously cloud his judgment in a dangerous way.

While keeping one eye on the house, Max occasionally checked on Mandy and James.

James appeared to be leading her to an area underneath a large tree, a hundred meters behind where Max lay on the ground.

The only thing Max could do was wait. He hoped Mandy was fine, and was worried about might have happened to her. Despite the non-starter status of their "relationship," and the mild bitterness between them, Max knew that he cared about her.

"Hey," whispered James, approaching Max from behind. "She's OK, but shaken up. And she needs medical attention. She's got a bad cut. She wouldn't tell me what happened, but I think she might have been attacked. Maybe you can get her to talk."

Attacked? Max wondered if there were already more people out there.

Max's mind was moving a mile a minute.

If there were more dangerous strangers around the farmhouse, then Max, Mandy, James, Sadie, and Georgia were all in grave danger. They had all their attention focused on the farmhouse, but now they might have to watch their backs as well.

Maybe a temporary retreat would be the safest thing. But that meant leaving Chad on the roof. Not to mention the gear that would keep them alive. They were already hungry.

"I'll go," said Max. "You stay here."

He handed the rifle back to James, who got into position on the ground.

Pain flared through his leg. Max moved slowly towards Mandy. He made sure to keep low to the ground.

"Mandy," he whispered, as he approached her. He didn't want to startle her.

Mandy sat cross-legged.

Blood was flowing freely from her hand. She still clutched a knife, a knife that Max recognized. It was one of his own, a Swedish carbon steel utility knife that had been in his Jeep forever, floating around the glovebox. He'd been glad that he'd remembered to take it after the accident with Georgia's SUV. Now it looked as if it had accomplished a purpose that it was never designed for.

Max wasn't sure, but he had a feeling that Mandy had killed someone.

Of course, Mandy would never kill unless she absolutely needed to. Unless there was no other option.

"Mandy," said Max, sitting down next to her. He winced in pain as he did.

Mandy didn't seem to notice his presence. She stared straight ahead.

It wasn't until Max put his arm around Mandy that she seemed to notice him.

"Mandy," said Max. "I need to know what happened. Can you hear me?"

Mandy nodded.

Max breathed a sigh of relief. She wasn't permanently shell shocked.

"What happened? Did someone attack you?"

"There was a woman..." said Mandy. "She looked... wild... like she'd gone wild... She came at me... I couldn't... I'm sorry... I had to..."

Max knew it was hard for Mandy. But he needed to

know the whole story. He needed to know if the woman was still a threat.

"Is she dead?" said Max.

Mandy nodded.

"You did what you had to do, Mandy," said Max. "Now let's have a look at that hand of yours."

Max took Mandy's bloodied hand in his own. Slowly, Mandy released her grip on the knife. Max took it delicately from her hand. He wiped it off on the cuff of his pant leg, and put it back into its plastic sheath on Mandy's belt.

"You're bleeding pretty bad," said Max. "This knife doesn't have a finger guard. I bet you let your finger slip forward and didn't even notice."

Max dug into his pocket for his own knife, a Spyderco Delica, full flat grind, and flicked it open. It had come with a pocket clip, but Max had removed it, knowing that people at his office would have disapproved of him carrying a knife. Without the pocket clip, it just floated awkwardly in the bottom of his pocket, usually lying horizontally. He wished he had that clip now.

Max cut a piece of his shirt off and tied it around Mandy's finger tightly.

"Hold the arm above your head for a while," said Max. "The bleeding should stop soon. You're going to be OK."

The two were silent for a moment.

Time was moving faster than Max had expected. The sun had set, and the world was now lit by the moon. It was a cloudless night, and the moon shone brightly.

"What's going on?" said Mandy. She seemed more alert now. "Why did James come and guide me away from the house?"

Max explained the whole situation to Mandy, as quickly as he could.

"So we're screwed," said Mandy. "All our provisions are in there. What are we going to do? We can't survive without that house, or our stuff."

"Not to mention Chad is still stuck on that roof," said Max. He told her how Georgia and Sadie were on the other side, with guns trained on the door.

"What if they leave through a window?" said Mandy.

"Shit," muttered Max. "I didn't think of that... Funny how your mind gets cloudy in these situations... I've got to remember that... I can't keep counting on the fact that I'm going to think clearly, no matter what."

"I doubt they'll go through a window," said Mandy.

"Hopefully not," said Max. "Anyway, maybe it'll work. After all, the idea is that they don't know we're here. They'll think we've simply abandoned the property."

"You were lucky not to get shot," said Mandy.

"Tell me about it," said Max. "Seems like I've been too lucky. Hopefully that doesn't mean my luck is about to change. What I'm worried about are the others... There are going to be more people coming. Like that woman you ran into. I don't know who she was. Maybe she was with the guy in the minivan, connected to him in some strange way. Or maybe she was a victim of these guys who are in our house. Who knows..."

"So what do we do now?" said Mandy.

"We wait," said Max. "We're just going to have to wait..."

"You think we can outlast the guys in the house?"

"Well, I hope so. If not, we'll have to come up with another plan."

"Hey, what's James doing? I thought he was supposed to have his gun on the door?"

Max suddenly saw it. James had his rifle clutched in just

one hand at his side. He was crouched low to the ground, moving swiftly towards the minivan.

That impulsive kid was going to ruin everything. And he was likely to get himself killed in the process, all while thinking he was doing the heroic thing.

10

GEORGIA

"How long do you think this is going to take?" said Sadie.

Georgia and Sadie were lying on their stomachs in some tall grass. Georgia had a straight shot to the front door. As well as some windows. She just hoped they weren't going to exit through the windows that she couldn't see.

"Could be a long time, Sadie," said Georgia, in a low voice. "Remember to speak quietly."

"I hope James and Max are OK."

Georgia didn't say anything. She was hoping the same thing. She didn't like having her kids separated from her, not in a situation like this. But she was going to have to get used to it.

"Can you see Chad?" said Georgia after a long pause, not taking her eye off the scope.

"Yeah," said Sadie. "He's still up there. He's not moving very much. Probably trying to stay quiet."

"I'm glad he had enough sense to kick the ladder down,"

said Georgia. "You know, if it wasn't for him, we wouldn't be in this mess."

"He's nice, Mom," said Sadie. "He's trying his best."

"Sometimes that isn't good enough," said Georgia. "Things are different now, Sadie. You've got to take this all seriously."

"I am," said Sadie. "I do my chores like everyone else. I keep a good watch. I'm getting better with a gun."

Georgia didn't say anything. She didn't know how she could instill in Sadie the attitude that she needed to have.

Georgia's thoughts turned towards the man that she had shot. It had left a sickening feeling in the pit of her stomach, one that she couldn't get rid of, no matter how much she told herself it was necessary.

But if given the chance, Georgia would do it again in a heartbeat. She was ready to shoot to kill. She wouldn't hesitate to pull the trigger when the time came. Not for those men. She'd heard them talk. She may not have known their names, but she knew what kind of people they were.

"Do you hear that?" said Sadie.

Georgia heard it. She didn't answer. She was too busy listening.

It was the sound of a car engine turning on. Georgia knew it must be the van. She hadn't heard any gunshots, so there couldn't have been a gunfight. It must have been Max or James moving the van out of the reach of the guys in the house.

"What's going on?" said Sadie.

"Shh," whispered Georgia.

Georgia was worried that the moving van might attract the attention of the men inside the house.

And she was right.

A moment later, she saw the door open.

Georgia had her eye glued to the scope.

A leg came out the door.

Georgia squeezed the trigger. She felt the kickback from the rifle, and her ears rang.

She'd fired too soon. She cursed herself. She'd literally jumped the gun. It was all the suspense of waiting, building up. But that shouldn't have affected her. She was used to hunting. But she still wasn't used to hunting people.

"You shot him!" said Sadie, much too loudly.

The man screamed in pain. He collapsed to the ground, falling out of the doorframe and onto the porch floor. He lay there, screaming, holding his leg.

Georgia waited and watched. She was holding her breath.

"Mom!" hissed Sadie, but Georgia ignored her.

Georgia was waiting to pull the trigger again. She was telling herself she was saving ammo by not firing and killing the man on the ground. She was telling herself that it was a strategic decision, that the second man might exit, and that she'd need to fire quickly to take him down.

But deep down, Georgia knew that she was hesitating because she didn't want to take yet another life.

She knew she had to do it.

Seconds ticked past. They felt like an eternity to Georgia. She had tunnel vision, and the sounds of the world around her had faded. Her ears rang, and she wasn't aware of anything but the man in her scope.

Georgia gritted her teeth.

She pulled the trigger.

The bullet struck him in the head.

Georgia breathed out.

Sadie didn't say anything.

No one else appeared in the doorway.

Two down, one to go.

A gunshot rang out on the other side of the house.

"Mom!" said Sadie, tugging on Georgia's arm. "We've got to get over there."

For once, Sadie had some good advice.

Georgia snapped herself out of it. She didn't look again at the dead man on the porch. She'd done what she'd needed to. She wasn't going to apologize to herself for it.

Georgia sprang to her feet.

"Come on," she said, taking Sadie's hand and tugging it. "James and Max need our help."

Part of Georgia wanted to stay back. Or to tell Sadie to stay back. She wanted to keep Sadie safe, but she also knew she might need her help in protecting Max, and more importantly, James.

11

JOHN

"I should have just stayed in my apartment," muttered John.

Lawrence, for once, didn't have a positive message to impart to John. He remained silent.

When they'd heard the chanting, John had led them further west to a bar that he'd frequented in his younger years. It was one of those trendy microbrew places that brewed its own beer.

John had gone there so much that he'd become friendly with the staff and eventually the owner. After one particularly intense late night session of drinking, John was forced to take the owner's keys away from him in order to prevent him driving home seriously impaired.

Because of what might be called an indiscretion on John's part, he never visited that bar again. He'd slept with the owner's sister, who was married at the time. The owner found out about it, and left a series of threatening voicemails on John's phone. John had never been the type to confront situations like that head on. He preferred to deal with the abstract world of numbers, focusing on his financial work and tuning out the world at large.

For some reason that he never could quite figure out, John had kept that set of keys. He'd kept them in his briefcase, toting them around every day. Maybe he thought that someday he'd get the guts to face the owner, who had been a real friend to him many times, and patch things up. But John never acted, and the keys became a reminder of his own cowardice.

The bar wasn't in the best neighborhood, and the doors were of thick steel, with good locks. But the key still worked, and the door opened for John and Lawrence.

They sat at one of the booths. Lawrence sat bolt upright, his hands folded on the table in front of him, as if he was meeting a new client. John slouched, his legs stretched out on the plush leather booth, his back resting against the wall.

A couple candles burned in front of them on the table. They had been hard to find in the near pitch-black bar. The moon was bright that night, but the bar had never been known for its windows.

Lawrence had drunk two entire large bottles of seltzer water, found behind the bar. John had drunk two as well, along with two beers. Now he was working on his third.

They'd been eating salted nuts constantly, and while they weren't ideal, they did slowly start to quench the raging hunger that John felt.

"So I don't get it," said John, suddenly turning his head and staring at Lawrence. "I don't get your whole deal."

"What do you mean?"

"I mean, you sound just so... This whole thing about helping people... It sounds like bullshit to me."

"And why do you think that?" said Lawrence.

"I don't need your therapist crap," said John. "Like I said, none of that matters now."

Lawrence shrugged. "I'm not trying to change your opinion about me," he said.

"Look," said John, taking a long sip from his beer mug. "I'm headed out of here. Out of the city. I'm probably going to die. But I think you should come with me."

"And why is that?"

"Because beneath all this 'helping people' crap, I know you really want to get out."

Lawrence shrugged. "I'm not sure I'm following you."

"Well," said John. "You came here with me, didn't you? Did you do that for purely altruistic reasons? I mean, what help have you provided me so far? Sure, you told me to get inside. That helped, but I'm pretty sure I would have figured that out myself. It's hard to miss that crazy chanting. It'd be hard to miss the screams..."

"Like I said, I've always been helping people. What I didn't say was that I always do the best job, or do the right thing... I haven't known how to approach this problem... Maybe I didn't do a good job, but who could?"

John studied Lawrence's face. He saw right through him, down to his core. He knew Lawrence wanted to get out, but that he didn't have the guts to do so. Instead, he was hiding behind his old identity, an identity that wouldn't serve him any longer.

John also knew that he himself had a greater chance of actually getting out if he had someone else there with him, someone to watch his back, someone to help him.

While John had spent most of his working hours staring at a computer, he'd also needed to meet regularly with clients and other investors. And he'd grown good at manipulating them. There was no other way to put it. He could call it anything he wanted, but he knew he was using well-defined tactics of manipulation. And John was the sort of person who was OK with that.

He could use those tactics on Lawrence.

If Lawrence really believed in his old professional identity, John would use that to his own advantage.

"Look," said John. "There's nothing you can do for the people here in the city. Everyone's going to starve to death, or who knows what. There are plenty of horrible fates that await them and you yourself. You can't help them. But if you get out... out to the countryside, there are going to be more survivors. There aren't going to be mobs there. There are going to be people who made it through, who haven't been sucked into this madness here... If you come with me, you could do much more good... I'm not asking for an answer now. Think about it. I'm leaving at dawn tomorrow."

Lawrence nodded, but didn't say anything.

John slept restlessly, as could be expected, but even so it was the best sleep he'd had in the last two weeks. The beer and peanuts had finally made his stomach actually feel full, and despite being buzzed, he felt he was regaining his strength.

The bar was on an out of the way side street, and there were no screams to be heard that night.

In the morning, John woke up feeling better than any day since the EMP, despite his mild hangover.

He started rooting around the bar, looking for things that could be useful. He gathered bottles of seltzer water, candles, lighters, and knives. Unfortunately, he didn't find the gun that had been rumored to be kept behind the bar.

"Hey," he said, prodding Lawrence. "You ready to go?"

John figured that if he posed the question this way, a "yes" was more likely.

"Uh, yeah," said Lawrence sleepily.

John didn't question him. He already had what he wanted from Lawrence.

"Help me get ready," he said. John gave Lawrence a rundown of what might be useful.

After twenty minutes, they had a pile of things laid out on the bar. Their weapons consisted of kitchen knives. Their food supply was nothing but nuts and limes. The milk in the mini fridge had long since spoiled. John filled some growlers with beer, saying the extra calories would be a help.

The next problem was trying to figure out how to carry it all. Lawrence had nothing useful, and all John had was his leather briefcase. Eventually, John found sacks of hops in the back. He slit them open with his kitchen knife, emptied out the smelly contents, and filled two of them with as much as he could. He handed one to Lawrence, who slung it over his back silently, and they were off.

John locked the door behind him, in case they needed to come back to the bar, in case the plan didn't work out.

John's mindset had changed yet again. He was starting to think it was possible that it actually all could work. He still knew it was a long shot... There was a long way to go just to get out of the city.

But if they could do it, get out past the dead-car traffic jams of the city and into the suburbs, he knew they could somehow find at least one working car with gas. There had to be one somewhere. All the city streets were gridlocked completely. There was no way to drive out.

"I still don't get how you survived out on the streets," said John, as they walked along the sidewalk. The sun was shining, and it would have looked like a beautiful normal day in Philadelphia. Except for the dead bodies that both

John and Lawrence ignored. And except for the cars abandoned on the road.

They passed some military trucks that were abandoned as well. Inside one of them, there was a soldier who looked like he had literally been torn limb from limb. Only a mob could do that. Not a single person. A group of people, acting together, like one giant animal.

"I don't know either," said Lawrence. "Then again, things have always worked out for me like that."

"So tell me what it was like," said John. "I literally didn't leave my apartment since it happened."

Lawrence started telling John all about the initial riots. He told John about the extensive looting. That was when people just thought the power was out momentarily. They thought it was going to come back on, and they wanted to get their money's worth, so to speak, by grabbing as many expensive goods as they could. Some, though, thought about water and food, and the grocery stores were empty within days.

Then the military came in, with their big rumbling trucks. They kept the city on lockdown, and imposed a curfew.

But as the days went by, and the power didn't come back on, the military and police were getting disorganized. They couldn't communicate with each other, and there was no one that they had to answer to. There were no higher ups. No word came from Washington. No word came from anywhere.

"And what happened after that?"

"Well, you saw the aftermath," said Lawrence, wincing at the painful memory. "Do I really need to go into detail?"

John didn't say anything.

"So how are you planning on getting out of the city

anyway?" said Lawrence. "You know if we manage to cross the river, there's still going to be about forty-five city blocks until we're out. Heading directly west, that is. And it's still dense after that. I doubt we'll be much safer once we reach Upper Darby."

"Remember," said John. "You're coming with me, so drop the whole 'how are you going to escape thing.'"

"Fine," muttered Lawrence.

"And the answer to your question is that I have no idea," said John.

They kept walking. The sun was at their backs, rising slowly over the apparently empty city.

Many of the bodies on the ground looked fresh.

"They must have been killed last night," said John.

Lawrence didn't say anything.

"Are you used to them or something? They don't seem to affect you. The bodies, that is."

"I don't know," said Lawrence. He seemed to be lost in his own head.

"Hey," said John. "Do you know of any boat rental places on the Schuylkill?"

"Boat rentals?"

"Yeah, you know, tourist traps? That sort of thing..."

"I think there was a paddle boat place. I haven't been down there in a few years, though."

"Perfect," said John. "That's going to be our out."

"What are you talking about?"

"Don't you see? We don't have to cross through West Philly. We're going to take one of those boats and leave the city that way... Who else is going to be crazy enough to be on a boat?"

Lawrence laughed nervously. "That's pretty crazy," he said.

"Well, do you have a better idea?"

"Did you hear that?"

"Hear what?"

It was too late.

A hand reached out and seized John. Or tried to seize him.

They had walked right past an alley and John had been so caught up in his plans that he hadn't even bothered to look in the alley. He had a lot to learn.

John turned, seeing his attacker for the first time. He was an overweight man, with a big belly. Like John, he wore business clothes that had become tattered.

For a second, John thought he recognized him. Maybe from some meeting long ago.

The attacker lunged forward, barreling towards John with all his weight. He collided with John, and they both fell to the ground.

The attacker grabbed John's hops bag, the bag full of food. It had fallen to the ground when John had been knocked down.

The attacker was up in a flash, moving quickly despite his size.

Lawrence lunged at the attacker, trying to grab him, but he merely grabbed the man's shirt. The man easily pulled himself free, and went dashing down the alley.

"Shit," said John, scrambling to his feet.

He knew that he needed that bag of food.

He also knew that he was lucky to be alive. Most people wouldn't merely tackle him for a bag of food, or unknown provisions. Most would kill first and examine the contents of the bag later. But this attacker was weak.

Just like John. He'd had the opportunity to stab the man when they were both on the ground. But he hadn't done it.

The knife had been in his hand the whole time, but he simply hadn't acted.

He wasn't about to make the same mistake twice.

Knife in hand, John dashed down the alley.

Lawrence ran clumsily after him. John heard the footsteps behind him, but didn't turn to look. He was intent on catching the thief and getting back what was his.

The alley opened up to 18th Street.

John turned the corner.

The attacker was resting against the brick wall of a building, the sack of food between his legs. He was panting heavily with exertion, and rummaging through the bag greedily. He didn't even look up to see John approaching him. He was too hungry, too desperate, to act sensibly. He was at his wit's end.

John walked slowly towards him, like an animal approaching its prey. He was angry, furious. His chest felt hot. Stealing someone's food was as good as killing them, thought John.

There was a sound off to his side, but John didn't look. He was too intent on the man rummaging through his food sack.

Something hard hit John in the shoulder. Pain flared through his body, and he fell to the ground. His head hit the pavement, and the knife fell with a clatter from his hand.

12

MAX

Max tried to ignore the pain in his leg, but it was almost impossible. He'd been using it far too much already. Now he was trying to run towards the house, away from Mandy.

James had been hotheaded enough to try to move the van by himself. What he hadn't considered was that since Max was with Mandy, it was James's responsibility to guard the door.

And apparently he hadn't thought that starting the van would cause the attackers to leave the house, to see what was going on.

A shot rang out on the other side of the house. There was nothing Max could do about it, except to hope that it was from Georgia. Likely, it was, since it was a single shot. But still, there was no way to know for sure.

The red rear lights of the van were on, and James was backing it up, moving it away from the house.

The door to the house flew open.

Max already had his Glock out. He raised it, ready to fire.

The attacker was raising his assault rifle.

Time seemed to move in slow motion.

Max felt a searing pain through his leg, and he suddenly collapsed to the ground, before even getting a shot off.

There was a noise as a shot was fired.

Max though he was a goner. He thought he'd be dead.

But he was still alive. His brain was still working.

He managed to look up, trying to ignore the pain in his leg.

The man with the assault rifle had fallen to the ground. He'd dropped his gun, and he didn't move.

The door of the van opened.

James got out, moving quickly to the man on the ground.

"He's dead," shouted James.

The pain in his leg was too much for Max. He shouldn't have been trying to run around on it.

Before passing out, Max vaguely remembered seeing Georgia and Sadie appearing. That meant that things were OK on their side—the gunshot Max had heard had been from Georgia, most likely. They were alive, and the attacker must have been dead. That was what mattered.

The last thing Max saw before his vision went black was Chad standing triumphantly on the roof, holding his rifle. It had been Chad. Chad, who everyone had thought was useless... he had saved the day.

Max woke up in almost as much pain as before.

He was back in the farmhouse, lying on his bed. He didn't know how much time had passed. It was dark outside. Candles lit the upstairs bedroom.

Mandy was sitting in a chair nearby.

"You're awake," she said, getting up.

"What happened?" said Max. "Is everyone OK?"

"Typical," said Mandy. "You want to know about

everyone else first. Don't you want to know if you're OK?" She was smiling at him as she spoke.

"I must have passed out from the pain," said Max.

"Your stitches came out," said Mandy. "It's amazing you did as much as you did with that wound."

"What about everyone else?"

"Well, as you can tell, we're back in the farmhouse. The guys who came in... they're both dead. Georgia shot one at the front of the house."

"You mean the back of the house."

"I'm going to let that slide, considering your condition."

"And Chad shot the other one?"

Mandy nodded at him.

"Where's everyone else? Who's on watch?"

"Georgia, James, and Chad are all outside."

"Don't tell me Chad's still on the roof."

Mandy shook her head. "Georgia's up there."

"I hope she got some rest or something to eat."

Mandy shook her head. "I gave her some more caffeine pills from the supplies."

"We're going to be running out of those soon enough," said Max. "I'm glad there are three people on watch. I don't know what we were thinking having just one person on the roof. It's clearly not enough."

"That's what we decided," said Mandy.

"I've got to go talk to them," said Max, starting to rise up in bed.

"It took me forever to get those new stitches into you," said Mandy. "You're not going anywhere. If you do, don't think that I'm going to stitch you up again."

Max grunted, but he sunk back down into the bed.

"Sadie's sleeping," said Georgia. "We can bury the bodies tomorrow."

"We need food," said Max. "Everyone's running on empty. I don't know how much longer we can last like this."

Mandy nodded. "Georgia said she had a deer in her sights before she saw the other men. There's food out there..."

"It's going to be tougher than I thought," said Max. "I guess I was naïve. I thought we'd just bunker down here, set up defenses for the occasional intruder, and that'd be that. But there are more people arriving than I'd thought, and sooner... Even if we can defend the farmhouse, it'd going to be too dangerous to hunt. And forget about growing food."

"What are you saying?" said Mandy.

"I'm saying we take that van and leave," said Max.

"Are you crazy?" said Mandy. "This is the only place we have. This is it."

"I know," said Max. "The farmhouse was my whole plan, but we need to get farther out."

"This is just your mania of getting to the absolute least populated area."

"Well, it worked so far, didn't it?" said Max.

"Fair point," said Mandy, bending over to examine Max's leg. "I wish we had those painkillers of Chad's."

"I'm fine," said Max, gritting his teeth. "That guy needed them more." Max was referring to the man who'd no longer be able to get his dialysis treatments.

"I don't get it," said Mandy. "What makes you think that anywhere else would be any better than here? You've been saying that the EMP must have hit the whole country, maybe even the whole world."

Max nodded. "Definitely," he said. "If it was just our area, we would have heard about it by now. They would have sent the army, or something."

"So the rest of the country is in the same condition? But you think it'll be better?"

"Think about," said Max. "We're just a day's drive from Philadelphia. And we're not that far from New York City. Two densely populated cities. And don't forget about the surrounding areas. It's not like everyone's been wiped out all at once. But if we can get farther out..."

"Where? Kansas? New Mexico? We don't even have maps. How would we even survive the journey?"

"The college kid who owned the van made it pretty far," said Max. "Maybe it's not that bad in the middle of the country. There are fewer people, and that means less chaos."

"I don't know," said Mandy. "What do you think the others would say?"

"I don't know," said Max. "They can stay here if they want. It'll be their house. It's not like property titles mean anything anymore."

"They all look up to you," said Mandy. And she added, in a softer voice, "And I do, too."

Max didn't say anything.

"We all know we wouldn't be alive if it wasn't for you," said Mandy. "Whatever you decide, everyone's bound to follow. Do you think we can get everyone in the van?"

"Yeah," said Max. "But I need to think about it. I need to talk to Georgia, too. And Chad."

"Chad?"

Max knew that Mandy had never had a high opinion of Chad. And apparently the fact that he'd shot the attacker hadn't changed her mind.

"Yeah," said Max. "He's traveled the country more than I have, probably more than any of us."

Mandy moved away from Max, headed towards the window. She stood there and looked out at the dark night.

"Are you OK?" said Max.

"My finger's fine," said Mandy. "It's just a cut. It'll heal."

"I don't mean your finger," said Max.

Mandy turned to look at him. She didn't say anything. But there was a far-off look in her eyes.

"It'll pass," said Max.

"I've never felt so bad about anything I've done," said Mandy.

"It was either you or her," said Max. "There was nothing else you could have done."

"That doesn't make it any easier."

"It doesn't have to," said Max. "You'll get used to it."

Max knew that it was likely that Mandy would have to kill again. He knew that they all probably would.

If they stayed at the farmhouse, they would kill and kill until they themselves were killed.

Max was embarrassed about the amateurish operation he'd been running here. There were no real defenses. A single person on the roof wasn't enough. Not nearly enough.

At least Max could now recognize his own weaknesses. His strategic weakness.

But if he wasn't good at defense, there were still things he was good at.

If they could get farther away, maybe they could thrive.

"Look," said Max. "I'm not saying we abandon the farmhouse forever. Maybe we just need to get away until things calm down more. Then we can turn it into a homestead. If we don't find something else better, that is."

"This was supposed to be the place to come to get away from it all," said Mandy.

"I know," said Max. "Trust me, I know."

Mandy didn't say anything for a moment. She continued to stare out the window.

"Do you ever think about the people you knew?" said Mandy.

"Sometimes," said Max.

"I do," said Mandy.

"It's only natural," said Max. "It's your brain trying to make sense of this all."

"How can you say that?" said Mandy. "You're saying my thoughts and worries aren't real?"

Max shrugged. "I don't know," he said. "I'm not really up for a philosophical discussion right now. We've got things to do. We've got plans to make, food and water to get before we're ready."

"Do you have any family?" said Mandy. There was a tone of annoyance in her voice. Max didn't know what it meant, but he wasn't about to get too concerned about it. There were more important things right now than people's feelings.

"Yeah," said Max. "I have a brother."

"And...?"

"What do you mean?"

"You don't think about him? You don't want to know what happened to him?" Mandy spoke like she wasn't going to give up without an answer from Max.

The easiest thing to do would be to answer her.

"I've barely talked to him in ten years," said Max. "I think he was pissed that I inherited the farmhouse. Not because he really wanted it. He had all the money he needed, and then some. He's a resourceful guy, and he always looks out for himself. It's one of his worst characteristics. Or it was. Maybe it'll serve him a lot of good now. I don't know."

"I have a sister..." said Mandy.

"Look," said Max. "We need to save our energy. We can't really get into this right now."

Mandy gave him a look that was more than mere annoyance. "How can you say that?"

The sound of a gunshot rang loudly outside, interrupting the conversation.

"Stay in bed," said Mandy. "Don't you dare move. I'll see what it is."

"At least hand me my gun," said Max.

Mandy was peering out the window. "I can't see anything. I'm going outside."

Mandy took Max's Glock and its holster from his clothing on the floor and handed it to him.

"Actually," said Max. "You should take it. You might need it."

"I have my rifle."

"Take it," said Max, holding out the gun and holster for Mandy.

She took it wordlessly, and left the room.

13

JOHN

"Are you OK?" said Lawrence, helping John sit upright, his back against the building.

"I think so," said John, wincing in pain. "That was some good work, scaring them off like that with the knife."

"I don't think I could have really stabbed anyone," said Lawrence.

"Well, you'd better change your mind on that," said John. "These guys were nothing compared to the others."

"Trust me," said Lawrence. "I know."

"Then you'd better get your head on straight. None of this helping people shit anymore. You've got to have an iron fist. Do we still have the bag?"

"Yeah," said Lawrence. "I've got it here. All the bar peanuts and limes we can eat."

John grunted. He held his head, not that it helped the pain.

"So you don't want me helping anyone, but it's fine that I'm helping you?" said Lawrence.

"We're helping each other," said John. "Remember?

You've changed your mind and realized you want to get out of the city."

Lawrence didn't say anything.

"Come on," said John, getting slowly and unsteadily to his feet. "We've got to keep moving. And keep an eye on the alleys this time."

They set off.

John's head was killing him, and he felt nauseous and weak, probably from the lack of proper food.

They walked the city streets for what felt like hours. It was the same almost everywhere. There were abandoned cars, trucks, police cars, and military vehicles. There were countless bodies on the ground.

They peered carefully into every alley as they passed it, not to mention every side street.

John tried to keep his guard up at all times, but it was difficult with his head hurting, battling the fatigue and nausea.

His feet were killing him. He was used to walking only a short distance to the office, or taking a cab when he had a business meeting, or a night out.

Lawrence seemed to be fighting the same fatigue. Occasionally, he held his lower back with both hands, as if it was hurting him.

"Just a little bit farther," John kept saying, over and over again.

Lawrence didn't say much. And John was glad that he'd dropped the whole "I only know how to help" attitude.

"I can't believe we haven't been attacked yet," said John, finally.

He'd practically been holding his breath the entire time, fearful that at any moment someone was going to simply shoot him, or jump out from behind an abandoned car and attack him.

John had never killed anyone before, and he didn't know if he had it in him.

"We're lucky," said Lawrence. "But at night, we won't be."

"I don't get it," said John. "It's like humanity here has gone nocturnal. It doesn't make sense. Why would everyone come out at night, if night is the most dangerous time? It's not like these people have lost all of their thinking and reasoning ability."

"Sometimes," said Lawrence. "Sick people on their deathbed become functionally nocturnal. Their circadian rhythm swings around when they're extremely stressed."

"You're saying that's happened to everyone here?"

"I don't know."

They walked in silence for another half hour.

"I know you're telling yourself," said John, "that you're going to try to help everyone out there in the suburbs or wherever. But we both know you're just trying to save yourself, which is fine with me. In fact, it makes more sense to me. Anyway, my brother Max, he's bound to be at this farmhouse. I know him. I know his thinking. I'm sure he's got it all fixed up to withstand the apocalypse. Hell, I wouldn't be surprised if he's set the place up like some impenetrable medieval fortress, booby traps and all. We can head there... Maybe he'll be glad to see me after all this time. And if not, I'm his brother, and he can't exactly not let me in."

"Let's cross that bridge when we come to it," said Lawrence. "First, we've got to get out of the city."

"Sounds like you're finally thinking sensibly," said John. "We're not that far from the boat rental place."

"Let's just hope there are still boats."

"Why wouldn't there be?"

"Who knows."

When they finally arrived at the river, they were exhausted. Almost by accident, they had arrived at exactly the right cross street, exactly where the boat rental place was located.

But there weren't any paddle boats, the small boats rented sometimes to tourists.

Instead, there was one large boat, bobbing gently in the water, tied up to a pier.

"Think the motor will work?" said John.

"I doubt it," said Lawrence. "Nothing works. Remember?"

"I'm going to give it a try, but I've got to eat something first. I feel like I'm going to pass out."

"Well, we've got limes and nuts."

"I'm going to go for the beer," said John, slumping down against a concrete wall.

"Don't you think we should get on the boat first?" said Lawrence. "And get under way?"

"What's the rush?" said John. "We'll see anyone coming."

"I don't know..."

"You've really changed your whole attitude," said John. "Now it's all about looking out for your own safety. As soon as I gave you the hope of getting out, everything changed."

Lawrence didn't respond. He seemed to have been growing more sullen all day.

John doubted that his own jabs at Lawrence's personality were helping at all, but he was too hungry and tired to care.

Lawrence sat down cross-legged on the ground, across from John.

They both opened up their sacks of hops, and started digging around for limes and nuts. John opened a growler of beer and drank greedily from it, trying to quench his thirst.

"Hey!" yelled someone, from not that far off.

"Shit," said John, rising rapidly to his feet. "Come on, get on the boat."

There were footsteps coming, pounding along the pavement.

John barely looked up. He saw two men running towards himself and Lawrence. One had a machete, and the other held a handgun.

John was rushing right towards the boat. Lawrence was only a few feet behind him. John could hear Lawrence's footsteps.

The boat was one of those clumsy tourist boats made for holding a lot of people, and certainly not made for speed.

John already suspected that the engine wouldn't start. And that was even if the keys were in there. And John had no idea how to hotwire a boat.

His only option was going to be to cut the boat free, and hope that he didn't get shot in the process.

John jumped onto the boat. His feet hit the metal deck of the boat hard.

Lawrence jumped, landing partially on John.

John was out from under Lawrence, moving as fast as he could on his hands and knees towards the rope that moored the boat.

John tried to keep his head down. He didn't want to get shot.

"Keep your head down," he yelled to Lawrence, but he didn't turn to look to see what Lawrence was doing.

With his expensive kitchen knife, John started hacking away at the rope. It wasn't as easy as he'd thought it would be. The rope was thick. But he finally cut through it. There wasn't a satisfactory snap like in the movies, but the boat was free.

He knew the men would be incredibly close.

The boat was already being pulled south by the current.

John poked his head above the crude metal edge of the boat. The two men were just arriving at the edge of the dock. It was too late for them. John and Lawrence were already drifting away. It was too far for the men to jump onto the boat.

But the man with the gun raised it.

There was anger in his eyes and on his face.

A shot rang out.

Lawrence screamed.

"Lawrence!" shouted John, turning around.

Lawrence was on the floor of the boat, bleeding from the torso. His face was pure agony.

John looked up. The man with the gun still held the gun straight and true. There was still anger on his face.

John didn't know how far a handgun could shoot. He scrambled behind one of the metal seats for tourists, trying to protect his body from subsequent shots.

Another shot rang out. But it didn't seem to hit anything.

John poked his head partially around the edge of the seat.

Lawrence was screaming in pain. They were floating down the Schuylkill River, heading south, which was the opposite direction John wanted to head. The sacks of food and beer lay on the dock, abandoned.

14

MANDY

"What happened?" said Mandy, rushing out onto the porch.

Max's Glock was in her hand, ready. Her rifle was strapped to her back.

"It's OK," said James.

"What happened?" said Sadie, emerging from the house behind Mandy, sounding sleepy and worried.

"Mom shot a deer," said James.

Mandy breathed a huge sigh of relief. "I thought there'd been another attack, or something," she said. "Max even lent me his gun."

"It's fine," said James. "We saw it heading right across the field. Looks like we're going to finally get to eat something."

As Mandy's eyes adjusted better to the moonlit night, she saw Georgia walking slowly across the field towards a dark lump on the ground that must have been the deer.

"I'll go help her," said Mandy. "Sadie, could you go tell Max what happened? He's probably going to be in there clutching a knife, waiting for the attacker."

"Sure," said Sadie sleepily.

"She needs to eat," said James, as Sadie disappeared inside, looking weary. "She's getting weaker."

"We all are," said Mandy. "Where's Chad?"

"He's on the other side of the house," said James.

"Good," said Mandy, nodding.

Although for some reason she didn't want to admit it to herself, it seemed as if Chad was really trying to pull his weight. Then again, he'd gotten in them so much trouble that Mandy figured Chad owed them all. And he hadn't exactly been much good on the roof until the very last minute.

Mandy started walking out towards Georgia. She kept the Glock out and ready, and she tried her best to keep her attention up. It was hard though, with her stomach begging for food, and her mind starting to wander with fatigue. She'd been awake for too long. They all had.

How were they going to get any rest when they had to work so hard just to defend the farmhouse? How were they even going to have time to find food and water, let alone eat it and drink it?

Maybe Max was right.

Maybe they had to leave.

Mandy tried to remind herself that she was still better off here than back in her apartment in the suburbs. Who knows what would have happened to her back there, if she'd stayed.

If Max hadn't broken down her apartment door, she'd most likely have died at the hands of those two criminals. And if she hadn't, maybe a worst fate would have awaited her.

"You finally had the chance to get one, eh?" said Mandy.

Georgia was already bending down over the deer, inspecting it.

"Finally we can eat," said Georgia, looking up at Mandy.

Even in the darkness, Georgia looked beyond exhausted. They had all been through a lot, but Mandy considered for the first time that maybe Georgia had it the worst of all of them. She was the only one who was really a decent shot at long range, so she held more responsibility for all their safety than anyone else. What's more, she had to worry about her two kids all the time.

That couldn't have been easy. Not in the apocalypse.

Mandy suddenly had a weird thought—that was the first time she'd called their situation "the apocalypse" to herself. Well, she supposed that it was true. It was the right thing to call it. Society had collapsed, and she doubted whether things would ever be the same. At least not for a long, long time.

"Here," said Georgia. "We'd better drag this to the porch. It's probably not safe to start dressing it here."

"Good call," said Mandy, grabbing one of the legs.

Together, they dragged the deer carcass back across the field.

"Nice shot, Mom," said James, when they got close.

Georgia seemed too tired to say much. She just nodded.

While they had the deer, they couldn't eat just yet. There was still a lot of work to be done.

Georgia took out a large folding knife from her pocket. The handle caught Mandy's eye for some reason. It was made of brass and wood. Mandy remembered her grandfather using one when she was a kid, but she didn't remember what it was called.

Georgia started to work, occasionally giving Mandy directions on how she could help.

Seeing the deer being cut open reminded Mandy all too vividly of the woman she'd stabbed. She tried to push the thoughts out of her mind. She felt like vomiting again, but she resisted. In the end, she was able to push through, and still manage to help Georgia. After all, getting the deer ready to eat had literally become a matter of life and death. She couldn't let her own feelings get in the way of eating.

"Max thinks we should leave the farmhouse," said Mandy, watching Georgia working with her knife.

"Leave the farmhouse?" said James. "Where would we go?"

"Make sure you're keeping watch, James," said Georgia.

"I am, don't worry."

"He thinks it's too dangerous here?" said Georgia, looking up at Mandy.

"Basically, yeah."

"He might be right. There were five strangers here in a single day. And we almost didn't make it."

"I know," said Mandy. "But don't you think that the numbers will... you know, die off? You know, as people... die off in the cities."

"Maybe," said Georgia. "But even if that happens, we've still got to stay alive here for days, if not weeks, while they keep coming. Frankly, I don't think we're going to make it that long."

"That's basically what Max was saying."

"Then again," said Georgia, taking a large piece of meat and laying it on the porch floor. "I don't know where the hell we'd go."

Mandy didn't know what to say. "Should we make a fire?"

"A fire will attract more people," said a male voice in the doorway.

Mandy turned around. It was Max, leaning against the doorway for support.

"What the hell are you doing out of bed?" said Mandy, growing angry.

"I wanted to make sure everything was OK," said Max.

"I sent Sadie in to tell you."

Max shrugged.

She could see in his face the pain his leg was causing him. Mandy couldn't believe how tough he was.

"You'd better at least sit down," said Georgia.

Max shuffled over to the swinging bench that hung from the porch roof.

"I think a fire is our only option," said Georgia. "The gas isn't working inside. We don't have another way to cook it. And we've got to eat."

"Could we eat it raw?" said Mandy.

"We could," said Georgia. "I've done it before. But we don't know what's in this meat. There could be parasites. I wish the gas stove inside still worked."

"We don't have the medication to treat it," said Max, from the bench. "Short term, it'd be good. Long term, though, it could be really bad."

"I think we should risk a fire," said Georgia. "We'll all have more strength if we've got some food in our stomachs."

She looked over at Max, who merely nodded.

"You have that fire starter?" said Georgia.

Max dug into one of his pockets and pulled out a fire steel, attached to a small lanyard.

There was already a piling of kindling and dead wood that Mandy had gathered a few days ago with Sadie.

Max pulled something else out of his pocket. "Here," he said. It was a small plastic tube that had once held film for a camera.

Georgia took the fire starter and the tube from Max. "Cotton balls?" she said, examining the tube.

"Soaked in Vaseline," said Max. "They'll ignite in almost any condition."

"Mandy says you're thinking we should leave."

"Yeah," said Max. "But we should talk about it after we eat."

"Does anyone have any water?" said Sadie, appearing once again on the porch. "I'm so thirsty I can't even sleep."

Mandy picked up her water bottle from where it rested against the side of the house. "Nope," she said, opening it up. "We'd better go get some. What do you think, Max?"

"Normally, it'd be better to wait until morning," said Max. "Someone could sneak up on you at night. But given the circumstances, maybe you should go. I'd go with you, but..."

"You're not going anywhere," said Mandy. "There's only so many times I can stitch you back up."

"Fine," said Max. "But you're taking Chad and James. Sadie, Georgia, and I will keep watch. Is that OK with you, Georgia?"

Georgia nodded. She was busy arranging the wood for the fire.

Mandy knew it was dangerous, heading out into the woods at night. But they needed water desperately. Her own throat was incredibly parched.

Mandy headed inside to fetch what was essentially a large plastic bag. She held one of the candles in front of her in order to see. Supposedly, it was better to use up the candles rather than the flashlight batteries. But either way, in a few weeks they wouldn't have candles or batteries.

The plastic bag was one of the emergency supplies that Max had brought along. Right now, it just looked like a smallish piece of folded plastic, but once filled with water, it could hold enough water for all six of them for a few days.

When Mandy got back to the porch, Georgia was already trying to spark the cotton balls. She had her folding knife out, and was striking the spine of the blade against the fire steel, sending sparks showering over the Vaseline-soaked cotton balls.

The cotton balls caught, and Georgia carefully lit pieces of bark on fire, in order to set the rest of the structure on fire.

Everyone seemed half-asleep.

Max looked at her sleepily. Suddenly, though, he seemed to momentarily become more alert.

"You checked the packs of the attackers, right?" he said.

Mandy immediately felt like an idiot.

"I didn't," she said. "And I'm sure they had water."

"It's OK," said Max. "We're making a lot of mistakes. And we've got to be aware of that, and figure out how to stay alive while we inevitably keep making them."

"I'll check the packs," said Mandy.

She went back inside the house to retrieve the packs. Georgia or Chad must have put them there in the living room, along with their assault rifles, which were leaning up neatly against the wall.

Mandy brought it all back outside.

She handed the guns to Max. "Maybe you'll know something about these."

Max began inspecting them, saying, "These could be useful. Very useful. This one's cheap, but it'll do."

Mandy dug through the packs, which were full of a hodge-podge of things.

Fortunately, there was water.

"Looks like the trip is off," said Mandy, feeling relief that she didn't have to head into the dark forest.

Max nodded.

Mandy gave Sadie a full bottle first, then took one to Georgia, then Max. And finally she herself took a drink.

Georgia already had the fire roaring, and she was using her knife to carve spits for the meat.

Her thirst finally quenched, Mandy went to help Georgia. Mandy worked to cut the meat into pieces that could fit on the spits. She used the same Mora knife she'd used to defend herself earlier. For the most part, she did a good enough job keeping those thoughts at bay.

Max hobbled over to the fire, and soon enough they were grilling meat. The smell alone was delicious.

Once the meat was ready, no one could wait long enough for it to cool down properly. They ate the chunks of venison directly off the spits. The meat burned Mandy's tongue, but she was too hungry to care.

"I'll go relieve Chad," said Mandy, getting up, after she'd scarfed down a few pieces of meat. Her stomach seemed to have shrunk in the last two weeks, and even when extremely hungry, she wasn't able to eat as much as she'd once been able to.

"Before you go," said Max. "Let's take a quick vote now that we've eaten. Who thinks we should leave in the van for greener pastures? The other option is to stay here, while more strangers arrive. Possibly very dangerous strangers. Raise your hand if you want to leave. Everyone gets a vote." He looked at James and Sadie as he spoke this last part.

Georgia raised her hand. "I'm with you, Max," she said. "I don't think we can last here. At least not until things calm down. Maybe we can head somewhere to hide out for a while before returning here."

"That sounds like a possibility," said Max.

In the end, they all voted to leave.

"I'll tell Chad," said Mandy. "It's not like his vote is going to make a difference anyway."

"I doubt he'll want to stay after being stuck on the roof," said Max.

Mandy felt better with food in her stomach, but she still felt like she was constantly on the brink of falling completely asleep.

Chad was patrolling the area in front of the house. She saw his figure moving in the moonlight, his rifle in front of him. He was trudging along, rather than walking. She could tell by his stride that he was dead tired.

Mandy had to admit that he now seemed to have something in him, something that made him keep going, no matter how bad things got.

"Chad," she called out, waving at him. She wanted to make sure she didn't startle him. If he thought she was a stranger, he might shoot her. Given the events of the day, it'd be understandable if he was a little jumpy and trigger happy.

"Hey," said Chad, approaching her.

His voice sounded incredibly weary.

"You feeling OK?"

"Sure," said Chad, but he didn't look OK. Even in the darkness, she could see that his eyes appeared sunken with fatigue.

Mandy explained the plan that Max had come up with.

"Wow," said Chad. "So what was this all for? Nothing?"

"What do you mean?"

"Defending this place, trying to keep it for ourselves. What was the point of it all?"

Suddenly, Mandy understood him. It made her feel empty and depressed. After all, they were headed yet again into the unknown. Would they ever find a place that was secure and safe? In only two short weeks, the farmhouse had come to feel like home for Mandy. Would she ever have that feeling again?

"Well," said Mandy. "I don't think we have much of a choice. Max is right. We probably won't survive if we stay here. Maybe we can come back. You'd better go get something to eat, Chad."

Chad nodded at her, and began trudging to the other side of the house.

Mandy was left alone in the darkness.

15

GEORGIA

They had decided to leave as early as they could. Rather than let everyone sleep before leaving, they'd realized it made more sense to leave as soon as possible, and then let themselves sleep in the van. They were all exhausted, and they all needed a lot of sleep. But with three people on watch, they'd have to take turns sleeping. It'd take forever that way, and they wouldn't be on the road before more strangers were likely to arrive.

Max was trying to do it all. He was trying to get everything in order. He was trying to figure out which provisions were crucial to take, and which weren't. After all, the van may have been big enough to fit all of them, but it wasn't big enough to fit all of them, plus all the gear, even considering the fact that they could attach quite a bit of it to the roof.

Max was currently rooting through the packs from the attackers, remarking on what would be useful and what wouldn't.

It was clear that Max was beyond exhausted. He'd been shot in the leg. He needed to rest.

"Max," said Georgia. "You can't do it all. If you want to be useful to us, you're going to have to live. And that means resting. Let us handle it. I don't know what we'd do if you died on us."

"I'm fine," said Max, but even his voice sounded exhausted.

Georgia knew that she wasn't going to be able to get Max to actually go to sleep. He wouldn't do it.

"Just handle the bags there," said Georgia. "I'll get the van ready. OK?"

Max nodded. He was smart enough to know what he couldn't do. Although sometimes, like everyone, he needed a reminder here and there of his own limitations.

Georgia had more strength in her now, her stomach full of the roasted venison. Everyone else was more animated too, although it was still going to be tough to get the van packed up and ready when no one had slept properly in who knew how long.

Georgia started delegating responsibilities. She told Sadie to head into the kitchen to see what she could scrounge up in terms of food and medical supplies.

They wouldn't be able to bring everything they had. The things that they had to leave behind, they would hide in the woods, in order to keep them from the people who would come by.

What Georgia would have liked to do was set up an area with free water and medical supplies for the people who would surely arrive. After all, not all of them would be killers or dangerous criminals. Many of them would be trying to keep their families alive, the same way that Georgia was.

But Georgia could barely feed her own family. There wasn't anything they could spare.

There simply weren't enough of them to do everything

that needed to be done. It would have been ideal to keep three people on watch while the rest packed. So many strangers had shown up yesterday that it was likely more would arrive soon. But the best Georgia could do was tell everyone to keep their eyes peeled and their guns ready as they went about their tasks.

Chad was in charge of carrying things to the van. With twine, he tied big things to the roof of the van, which fortunately was equipped with a metal roof rack, making it easy to attach things.

Georgia had already examined the van. It wasn't perfect, but it would do. It had almost a full tank of gas. The engine started, and it sounded fine when it ran. There was a full sized spare tire in the back, underneath the carpeting.

James was going between Max and Chad, handing things that Max took from the packs to Chad. The items were piling up outside the van, and soon there'd be simply too much to fit. They'd have to make difficult choices about what to bring.

The sun was starting to rise. Georgia was hoping to get on the road before 9 o'clock, but she didn't know if that was going to happen.

The whole situation reminded her somewhat of going on vacation with her kids, trying to get the truck ready at the last minute.

Of course, they weren't heading on a vacation at all.

And the reality of the fresh dead bodies on the farmhouse property couldn't have underscored that fact more.

"Mandy," said Georgia, pulling her aside from what she was doing. "We've got to do something about the bodies."

Georgia shook out another two caffeine pills from the plastic bottle she carried with her. Soon it would be empty. But for now she needed to stay as alert as possible. She handed one to Mandy, and swallowed the other one herself.

"Are you sure?" said Mandy. She looked like she didn't like the idea.

"Well," said Georgia. "No, we don't have to. But it seems like the proper thing to do. We don't have time to really bury them."

"What are we going to do with them?"

"Drag them to the woods," said Georgia matter-of-factly. "Cover them with some leaves."

Mandy seemed to be considering it. "Have you asked Max?"

Georgia shook her head. "Honestly, I think he'd want to leave them out as a warning or something, trying to discourage people from coming to the house. But it doesn't seem right to me."

"You think he'd really want to do that?" said Mandy.

"I don't know," said Georgia. That was the truth. Max certainly wasn't cruel. But he was very practical minded, and almost ruthlessly pragmatic in his efforts to protect the group.

"All right," said Mandy. "Let's do it."

"Come on," said Georgia.

It was almost startling how everyone had so quickly learned to ignore the dead bodies on the ground. On the side of the house with the van, there were three, all from yesterday.

First, they went to the young man, the former owner of the van. His eyes were open, and Georgia leaned down and closed them gently. His body was already stiff from rigor mortis.

"We're going to have to drag them," said Georgia. "If we carry them all, we'll be exhausted."

"I'm not sure I can get any more exhausted," said Mandy.

"We'll get to sleep in the van," said Georgia. "We'll leave soon enough. We just need to push through for a little while longer."

"That's what I've been telling myself," said Mandy. "But more and more things keep cropping up. It seems like we're never going to get a chance to rest. I thought we were safe once we got to the farmhouse. I was so happy we were all safe."

"That's the way it works sometimes," said Georgia. "But we'll get there eventually."

"But who knows what awaits us on the road," said Mandy. "It could be even more dangerous where we're headed than here. And we don't even have a plan. That's what worries me."

"Max thinks that if we head far enough west, we'll be safer. Remember those population density maps of the US? I think he's right. Plus, this clueless college kid got halfway across the country fine. He didn't have any weapons, or even a sense of self preservation, apparently."

"I guess we don't really have any other options anyway," said Mandy.

"Nope," said Georgia. "It doesn't look like it. Now I guess we can take a leg each."

"It's not very dignified," said Mandy, reaching down and grabbing the stiff leg.

"The apocalypse isn't very dignified," said Georgia. "We don't have control over so much. We've got to make the best decisions for the things that we can control."

Together, they dragged the young man to the woods.

"That's a nice spot over there," said Mandy, pointing to a spot between two large trees.

Georgia wasn't even thinking about *where* the young man should be laid to rest. She was keeping her eyes out for any strangers that might be approaching. She was ready to grab her gun in an instant.

"That's fine," said Georgia.

They dragged the body a little farther, and then covered him with some dead leaves from the forest floor.

"One down," said Georgia.

"Uh, Georgia," said Mandy, as they walked back to the farmhouse. "Maybe someone else can help you with that woman... I just..."

Georgia knew Mandy'd had trouble with killing to defend herself. But she also knew that it wasn't something that Mandy could avoid.

"Nope," said Georgia. "You're going to help me with her. And we're doing her next. The faster you confront your feelings on this, the better off you'll be. Trust me. It's going to help you in the long run."

Mandy didn't say anything, but she walked with Georgia to where the woman's body lay, her throat slit, stab wounds on her torso, dried blood everywhere.

"Come on," said Georgia. "You can do it."

"I feel like I'm going to throw up again," said Mandy, turning away from the body.

"Come on," urged Georgia. "You did the right thing. You defended yourself. You can't let this experience make you hesitate in the future."

Mandy turned back around, and stared right at the dead woman's face.

Good, thought Georgia to herself. Mandy was making progress.

Together, they dragged the woman to the woods. This

time, Mandy didn't suggest any particular place for the "burial" site.

Next were the three attackers. By the time they were done, they were too tired to cover the bodies with leaves.

"They tried to kill us anyway," said Mandy. "I'm not sure they deserve to be covered."

Mandy and Georgia were both panting with exertion, and they had to sit down in the woods to recover their strength.

"The van should be almost ready," said Georgia. "But they might need help figuring out what to leave behind."

"Any idea where we're headed?"

"West."

"I mean, more specifically."

"I don't know," said Georgia. "I've never been out of Pennsylvania."

"Really?"

"Well, I've been down to the shore, stuff like that."

"I haven't really traveled much either. I visited a friend in San Francisco once. Of course, I drove."

"I don't think we have any maps that aren't just for Pennsylvania," said Georgia.

"Great," said Mandy. "Why do I get the feeling that each step we take is like two steps backwards? It's like we're getting less prepared with each passing day."

"Yup," said Georgia. "I know the feeling. But there's no point in dwelling on it. Come on, we've got to move.

Georgia stood up and offered Mandy a hand, helping her up.

"You sure sound like Max sometimes."

"I'll take that as a compliment," said Georgia.

"Hey," whispered Mandy suddenly, tugging on Georgia's arm. "Do you see that over there?"

Georgia looked where Mandy pointed.

In the distance, between the trees, there was a hint of movement. Whatever it was, it was too far off to see clearly.

But Georgia was familiar with how animals moved. This definitely wasn't an animal.

That meant it was a "someone."

16

JOHN

The tourist boat was floating down the Schuylkill River, headed in the wrong direction.

Lawrence had died on the crude metal floor. He'd bled to death. John had held him until the end, silently. There was nothing that could have been done. The tourniquet John fashioned from Lawrence's shirt didn't work. The wound was too massive.

Now John was covered in Lawrence's blood.

As the time passed, John began to partially recover from the shock of losing the man who had become his unlikely friend. His mind returned to practical matters, and he realized that he had no food, no water. His only possessions were his blood-stained clothes and his kitchen knife. If anyone saw him, he'd look like a knife murderer from a horror movie.

At some point, John decided that a burial at "sea," or in this case, the river, was the best burial that the former therapist was going to get.

It took quite a bit of effort to hoist Lawrence's body over the side of the boat. John had needed to get almost entirely under Lawrence's body and push upwards. Then Lawrence's belt had gotten caught on the rough lip of the boat's side. It had taken what felt like an eternity to solve that problem. Finally, with a huge final push, Lawrence was overboard, landing with a splash in the Schuylkill.

John was trying his best to think clearly. It was difficult with his pulse racing from the physical exertion, not to mention the anxiety produced by the situation.

He was sweating, and he didn't have anything to drink. His throat was already parched. His hair stuck to his forehead and his shirt stuck annoyingly to his back.

John took a deep breath and sat down in one of the boat's seats.

He closed his eyes, trying to ignore his surroundings. He tried to picture where the Schuylkill River led. Eventually, he knew, it fed into the larger Delaware River, which ran south, past Delaware, eventually leading into the Atlantic.

John knew he needed get off the boat soon. He certainly wasn't going to stay on it until the river got wide. And he certainly wasn't going to float all the way to the Atlantic. He needed to make his move soon, while he could still see the shore.

Thoughts of Lawrence's death kept poking at his mind, distracting from the plans he needed to make. The death was just so senseless. The men had already been enough of a threat that John and Lawrence had fled onto the boat. The men essentially already had all the food they'd be able to steal from John and Lawrence, in the abandoned sacks on the dock.

Maybe there was another reason. John knew he shouldn't have been thinking about it now, but he couldn't help it. Maybe the men had been the owners of the boat. He hadn't even considered that possibility until now. But still, the boat was already gone. Their only motive could have been revenge.

John had always looked out for himself. But in this instant, he felt that he should have been the one who'd been shot. After all, hadn't the whole thing been his idea? Lawrence didn't deserve this. He should have stayed in the city. But John had convinced him to leave.

Then again, Lawrence would have died for sure in the city, one way or another. That much was certain. Almost everyone there would die, sooner or later. There simply wasn't any food being grown. The animals weren't big enough to survive for long. John didn't want to think about the possibility of cannibalism. And still, that would only work for so long.

He had to snap out of it.

John shook his head back and forth like a dog.

He was studying the banks of the river, trying to figure out where he was.

It looked like he was somewhere in the sprawl of Southwest Philly. This wasn't exactly where he wanted to be, but at least here he wouldn't have to travel through the densely populated West Philly neighborhood.

It was now or never, figured John. In a couple minutes, he might not have the mental energy to even try to escape. And who knew, maybe the river would become more rapid. The longer he waited, the farther he'd get from the farmhouse.

Not that he'd ever get there.

John knew he needed to bring the knife with him, but he didn't relish the idea of swimming with it. Then again, he couldn't think of anything to do with it.

John acted suddenly. He intentionally didn't give himself time to think about the consequences.

He hurled himself over the side of the boat completely unglamorously.

He fell with a splash into the water. It was colder than he'd thought it would be.

John didn't look back. He swam, as best he could, with the kitchen knife in his hand. He'd been a competitive swimmer back in high school, but that was a long time ago, and he found himself tiring quickly.

The bank of the river hadn't looked far from the boat. But now, with his eyes just a few inches above the water, it looked almost impossibly far.

John's form was getting looser the more fatigued he became. He wasn't aware of where his hands and feet were moving. The only thing he knew was that he had to keep moving them. He had to keep going.

Suddenly, he felt a pain in his side.

It took a moment for him to realize what had happened.

Somehow, he had let the knife swing too close to his body. And it had cut him.

He didn't know yet whether it was a simple nick, or a deeper wound. It wasn't like he was able to check it, there in the water.

John tried to keep the knife out of the way as much as possible as he continued.

The pain wasn't too bad. But it worried him.

But the only thing he could do was to keep going.

17

CHAD

The van was packed. Mostly. Chad had spent all morning carrying all the heavy stuff to the van and trying to figure out a way it could all fit inside. And that was counting on six people being in the van.

A huge pile of provisions lay next to the van. Everyone should have been working together to figure out what was absolutely crucial, what they *really* needed to bring. But everyone was so tired, and there was so much to do, that in the end a lot of the decisions were left up to Chad and Chad alone, since he was the one actually loading the van.

Chad's muscles ached from the effort. He'd been getting fitter since arriving at the farm. But he still had a lifetime of inactivity behind him. It would take more than two weeks to catch up.

On top of the muscle soreness, Chad was simply exhausted. It wasn't like the others had had any rest either. But Chad had spent all that time on the roof. It'd been probably the most stressful event of his life.

He'd frozen up when he'd seen the attackers for the first time. He'd gotten one in his sights, but the guy'd been running. And Chad had just kept waiting until he thought he could really get the shot. He knew that he wouldn't be able to fire another shot in quick succession, so he'd kept waiting for the perfect shot. And that shot never came.

The others, Max, Georgia, and everyone—they probably thought Chad was worthless. After all, he was the one who'd been on watch. It'd all been his responsibility. If it hadn't been for Georgia, who knew what would have happened.

Chad kept his eyes peeled as best he could, walking around to the other side of the house, to tell Max that the van was almost ready.

He heard footsteps running off to the side, by the woods. It was Georgia and Mandy, their rifles held in their hands.

"Chad," said Mandy, using a loud whisper when she got close. "People. In the woods."

Shit. This was the last thing they needed.

Georgia and Mandy didn't stop running, and they motioned for Chad to follow them around to the other side of the house.

Chad lumbered along behind them, running as best he could, keeping his eyes fixed on the woods that they'd come from.

"What are we going to do?" said Chad, panting.

"We've got to get on the road now," said Mandy.

"How many of them are there?"

"We don't know. Saw a couple."

"Max," said Georgia, running up the wooden stairs of the porch. "Max, wake up."

Max woke with a start. He instinctively reached for his Glock and had it in his hand before his eyes were fully open.

"We've got to hit the road, Max," said Georgia. "Mandy and I saw people in the woods. More than one. No idea who they are."

"Shit," muttered Max, closing his eyes, as if he was thinking hard.

"We don't have the energy to fight them," said Georgia. "We're all dead tired."

"Yeah," said Max, opening his eyes again. "Realistically, we're not going to win, especially if they're intent on taking the house. Better to just let them have it. We're not going to make it through another day like yesterday."

"But we're not done packing," said Chad. "I've got a lot of stuff in the van, but there's plenty more I couldn't fit in. If we left now, we'd be leaving a lot behind. And I mean a lot. I thought you would all want to go through it once more."

"We can't be cowboys about this," said Max. "We've got to leave now, whether we're packed or not."

Everyone else was nodding their head, in agreement with Max.

Maybe Chad was just exhausted, but in his mind, the provisions were more important than risking another gunfight.

"Look," said Chad. "Say we get out of here without getting shot, what good is it going to do us if we've left something critical behind?"

"You were the one packing the van," said Mandy. "Let's hope you did a good job."

"Come on," said Max. "We can't discuss this any longer. How close were they?"

"Pretty close," said Georgia. "And getting closer."

Max stood up, gritting his teeth in pain.

Chad moved over to help him up.

"I'm fine," said Max. But it was clear his leg was killing him.

The group cut through the house, taking one last look around for anything that they might need to grab. Chad stuffed a couple unused candles in his pockets. Not to mention a few pieces of cooked venison that were lying out on some newspaper.

"You're driving first, Chad," said Max, as they approached the van.

"I really hope we don't need any of this, Chad," said Mandy, eyeing the pile of left-overs on the ground. She spoke his name with disdain.

Truthfully, Chad could understand Mandy's occasional disdain for him. How many times had Chad and Chad alone been responsible for almost getting them all killed? That didn't mean it didn't bother him. He wasn't like Max. Things didn't just slide right off of him. He felt everything. People used to tell him that he was too sensitive. Maybe that was why he'd gotten mixed up in drugs in the first place. The first time he'd popped a Vicodin, he felt all that sensitivity and anxiety just slide right off of him. Now, without the drugs, it was like he was entering the world again for the first time.

Chad got behind the wheel, and the rest clambered inside. The van technically seated eight, and there were six of them. The remaining seat, the one in the back right, Chad had piled high with gear. He'd stuffed things under the seats, and in the foot spaces. He'd put knives in the glove box and bandages in the pockets behind the seat. Everything was completely disorganized, a necessity of trying to fit it all in.

Chad closed the door behind him, his hand reaching for the keys which had been left on the dash. He suddenly realized that there was a small chance that the van wouldn't start. He didn't know why, but he had a horrible anxious feeling in his solar plexus, a tightness that would barely let him breathe—what if the van didn't start?

"What are you waiting for?" came Mandy's voice from the behind him.

"Let's get a move on it," said Georgia, in the passenger seat.

Max was in the way back, his eyes seemingly glazed over with pain. James and Sadie were completely silent. They seemed just as nervous as Chad.

Chad turned the keys.

The engine started.

He didn't yet breathe a sigh of relief, though.

"There they are," said Mandy, her voice rising in terror.

Chad looked off towards the woods.

Half a dozen figures or so were emerging from the trees. He couldn't get a good look at their faces. They walked in a pyramid-style formation. The way they moved alone made Chad think of the military. They had large guns with them, held with the muzzles pointed down. Most of them wore camouflage clothes. Something about the way they moved made them seem… professional.

Chad knew one thing. You don't want to run into professionals during the apocalypse.

After all, what would their profession be? Killing?

Chad was frozen in fear. His hand was on the shifter, his foot on the brake.

"Go!"

"Chad!"

Everyone was urging him to move, to drive. But it was as if he couldn't get his body to respond. He couldn't make himself even shift the van into reverse.

"Come on!" said Georgia, tugging on his sleeve.

Finally, after what felt like an eternity, Chad snapped out of it.

He put the van in reverse, spun the wheel, and hit the

accelerator. Chad spun the van around, pointing it towards the road.

"They see us," said Georgia.

"Are we going to be OK, Mom?" said Sadie.

"We're going to be OK, Sadie," said James.

"Go!"

"Go!"

Chad wasn't sure who was shouting in the van.

He slammed the van into drive, and jammed his foot down on the pedal. The tires spun in the loose earth, and they were off, heading towards the road down the long, winding driveway.

Chad looked briefly in the rear view mirror. The men in formation were out of his sight.

There were no dramatic gunshots. No one shot at the van. No one ran screaming at them.

But the silence was almost worse. Because it meant too many unknowns.

The farmhouse was now in their past. What they had left behind was now gone, and it was unlikely it would be safe to return. Max had been both wrong and right—it'd been a safe haven for what felt now like a brief moment. And it had quickly become too dangerous. They were too close to the cities, to civilization.

They needed to get far, far away, to some unknown and unpopulated lands.

"Who were they?" said Sadie.

No one answered. Because no one knew.

The only thing that seemed certain was that the men weren't friends. They'd come to take what they needed, and it wasn't likely they'd be kind. Not with those guns in their hands, not with the way they moved.

"Here," said Georgia, shaking out a caffeine pill and holding it out for Chad. "It's the last one."

"Thanks."

"You OK to drive?" said Georgia. "We'll take shifts. That way everyone can get some rest."

"Not really," said Chad. "But what choice do we have?"

"Right," said Georgia. "I'll stay up with you. Everyone else, get some sleep." She turned her head around to address the rest of the group. "You hear me?"

Chad looked in the rear view mirror, adjusting it. James and Sadie had already fallen asleep, passed out cold, their heads tilted to the side and their mouths open. Max had fallen asleep as well. His injury must have really exhausted him, because it wasn't like Max to let himself sleep while others kept him safe.

Chad felt a moment of panic. If Max didn't make it, what would they do?

But this wasn't a good time to worry about that, and Chad knew it.

Only Mandy remained awake, but she was looking out the window with a far-off look in her eyes. She wouldn't be awake for long.

"Here goes nothing," muttered Chad, as he slowed the van down to take the turn onto the road. The gate was already open. The original owner of the van had left it that way.

The tires of the van ran smoothly along the paved road.

It was strange to be driving the van on a paved road. It almost felt like the EMP had never happened, and society had never collapsed. After all, the driver's seat was upholstered and comfortable. And there was air conditioning and even a radio. Not that the radio would work. And not that they'd use the AC, since it would use up far too much gas.

"Let's hope this goes well," said Georgia. "Who knows what we're going to find out here."

"We don't even know where we're headed," said Chad.

"Max said you'd traveled west, right?" said Georgia. "I think he thought you were going to be our guide, since we don't have any maps for the other states."

"Are you serious?" said Chad.

"Yeah, that's what he said."

"I mean, I've bounced around a little, yeah," said Chad. "But it's not like I know the routes or anything. I usually took the bus... One time, I made a road trip to LA in an old jalopy that a friend lent me... To be honest, I was out of it most of the time. The only thing I remember is that the roof was caving on me."

"You drove high?" said Georgia, disdain filling her voice.

"Uh, yeah, wasn't my proudest moment."

"Sounds like you haven't had a lot of those."

"Not really. Nothing I can do about it now, though."

"You're doing good, Chad," said Georgia.

He looked over at her briefly, and she looked at him.

He knew she was referring to his effort to be responsible, to look out for the others, to do more than his fair share of the chores back at the farmhouse.

Georgia wasn't the sort of woman to throw out excessive compliments. So, coming from her, it was kind of a big deal. Especially since Chad already felt like he'd screwed up so much at the farmhouse.

Chad drove on. Mandy had already fallen asleep, along with the rest of them. He and Georgia didn't speak for the next half hour.

Being out on the open road was the strangest thing. The sun was shining, bright and cheery, and the country road couldn't have looked more peaceful. The leaves on the trees were bright and green. It would have been a beautiful, relaxing drive, had the situation been entirely different.

Chad tried not to let his mind wander. But he couldn't help it. He tried his hardest to think of practical things. They needed to know where to go, first of all. And they'd need food, not to mention water. And of course gas. They couldn't go anywhere without that. They had just one tank. One pitiful little tank. Who knew how far that would take them, with six people in a fully-loaded down van that couldn't have gotten the greatest gas mileage to begin with.

Chad couldn't focus on any of that.

Instead, he found himself reminiscing about a trip he'd taken when he was younger, the year before he'd gotten involved in drugs. If he was being honest with himself, it was one of the last truly coherent memories he actually had. It'd been a hiking trip with the local camping group, and they'd headed up to the Poconos, where beautiful pine trees lined a small man-made lake. There wasn't anything really exciting that had happened on the trip. It was more that there'd been a certain *feeling* he'd always associated with that area. It was the feeling of peace and calm... Chad had no idea why he was thinking about it now.

Max was injured. Everyone else was asleep. Georgia may have been there, but Chad was driving. And he was just as fatigued as the rest of them. He wasn't ready for this level of responsibility. He just wasn't that kind of guy, and he knew it.

Why couldn't it have been Chad that'd been shot, rather than Max? He certainly wouldn't have relished being shot. Or the ensuing pain. But he didn't deserve this responsibility.

Max had been injured because he'd stuck his neck out

for all of them. Chad hadn't done so, though. So there wasn't any more to think about.

"Chad!" said Georgia, sounding frantic. "What are you doing?"

That snapped Chad out of his daydreaming and thinking.

His eyes had been on the road, but he hadn't really been focusing.

Suddenly, Chad saw it.

In front of them, on the long stretch of two-lane country road, there was a roadblock.

It was nothing more than some tree trunks that lay across the road.

If they collided with it, the van would be toast, and they wouldn't have a vehicle, arguably one of their most important tools for survival.

Who'd put those logs there? Were there people lying in wait?

And if they couldn't get through here, where were they going to go? There'd been no other roads since leaving the farmhouse driveway.

There was no time to worry about that now, though.

If only Chad had noticed it earlier.

He slammed on the brakes.

But the van was rapidly heading towards the logs.

18

MAX

The last thing Max remembered was leaving the farmhouse. He'd passed out into a deep, dreamless sleep from which he remembered nothing.

Next thing he knew, everyone was shouting.

Max's eyes were open in an instant. Up ahead was a rudimentary roadblock made of tree trunks dragged into the road. If that college kid had gotten through, coming from the west, then that meant the roadblock was new. Brand new. That meant there was someone there.

Shit, this wasn't good.

It'd looked like they'd crash into it. But Chad slammed on the brakes just in time, and the van came skidding to a stop.

"What do I do?" said Chad, sounding frantic and worried in the driver's seat.

"Keep your heads down," said Max.

Everyone did as he said.

"Guns as ready as you can get them," said Max. "Or knives."

It'd be hard to get their rifles ready in the confines of the cramped van. But if it came down to it, they could open the windows and stick the rifles out. If it really came down to it, they'd open the doors and get behind them for shelter.

Max's hand was already on his Glock.

His leg was killing him, but he'd ignore it as best he could. He was pretty sure he could walk again now. He'd gotten enough rest. For now, at least.

And if he could walk, he could fight. Maybe not as effectively as before. But he'd do it.

Max was scanning the surrounding area through the slightly-tinted windows of the minivan.

"Should I turn around?" said Chad frantically.

"Not yet," said Max. "Keep the engine on."

"Shouldn't I turn around?"

"Not yet," said Max.

This time, Chad listened.

In the row of seats in front of him, Max saw Mandy reaching for her Mora knife. She pulled it from the plastic sheath.

That was good, thought Max. It meant Mandy was already getting over having killed that woman in self defense. If they lived through this incident, it would serve Mandy well. It would serve them all well. No one could afford to hesitate when defending themselves.

"We didn't pass any other roads," said Georgia. "There's no other way."

That was exactly what Max had feared.

"We'd have to head really far east, then north, before we could go west again," said Mandy. Her hand was clutching her knife handle. "We'd use up too much gas..."

Max knew she was right. She'd spent more time with the maps than anyone else.

The whole area was getting overrun with people. They

needed to get out. And fast. They couldn't waste time driving east, even if they weren't factoring in the gas. With the gas, they might never get out.

It was either get through this roadblock, or die trying.

There was no other way.

"I think I should turn around," said Chad. "There's got to be someone out here..."

"Don't turn around, Chad," said Max. "Don't even think about it. Everyone, we're going to have to get through this roadblock. Keep your eyes on the trees. Try to see if there's any movement."

They hadn't been shot at yet. That seemed like a good sign. But it didn't mean much. After all, if the roadblock creators intended to steal vehicles, for instance, it wouldn't do them much good to shoot at them. They'd destroy the van in the process, rendering it useless for themselves.

No. If someone wanted the minivan, they were going to come close and take it by force, doing as little damage as possible to the vehicle.

Well, let them try, thought Max.

He gritted his teeth against the pain in his leg.

"What do we do?" whispered Mandy.

"We wait," said Max. "Everyone, keep as silent as possible. Keep your heads down. They might shoot at the windows."

Everyone fell silent. The time started to tick by. Impossibly slowly.

No one appeared. No movement.

"Maybe we should get out and move the logs," whispered Chad. "Maybe they're there by mistake?"

"No chance," whispered Max.

"Yeah," whispered Georgia. "Tree trunks don't move themselves."

"Well, maybe they put them there and left. Whoever they are."

"Why go to all that work?" said James, speaking too loudly.

"James," whispered Georgia. "We've got to stay quiet."

"Sorry," whispered James.

"Look," whispered Sadie. "Over to the left."

She had her head down as low as she could get it in her seat, and she was pointing off towards one of the trees.

Max saw it. A flash of movement.

"I hope it's not the militia-style group we saw back at the farm," whispered Georgia.

No one responded. Max was studying the trees where Sadie had seen someone. A full minute went by, and then another, and there was nothing.

But someone was out there, hiding in the trees.

Finally, the person in the trees moved again. This time, Max got a better look.

"It's a woman," whispered Max. "And she's wearing civilian clothes."

"Armed?" whispered Georgia.

"No rifle that I can see," whispered Max.

"See anyone else?"

"No."

"This is killing me," said Chad. "We've got to do something. We've got to turn back, or try to go through."

"Hold on, Chad, hold on."

"Another one!" said Sadie, forgetting to whisper.

Max looked where she was pointing, to the other side of the minivan.

This time, there was no doubting what he saw.

It was a man, big and burly, wearing a dirty workman's jacket, jeans, and boots. He was close enough to see his face, which was red and weather-beaten. He was in his mid 40s, and looked like he'd spent a lifetime working outdoors. He carried a shotgun, the sights raised to his eyes.

Max didn't know why, but there was something in the man's face that seemed trustworthy. He didn't have a hint of malice in his eyes. Not that you could tell a book by its cover. Certainly not these days.

"Keep your eyes on the other side," whispered Max.

"What do I do?" said Chad, speaking at full volume again out of nervousness.

"Nothing," said Max. "Keep your eyes peeled. I'm getting out to talk to this guy."

"Are you crazy?" said Mandy. "He's got a gun."

"I'm going to see if I can negotiate," said Max. "We're not going to shoot someone just because he has a gun. Not until he's a threat, that is. Chad, if things go wrong, get everyone out of here. Turn the van around and drive fast."

Before anyone could protest, Max was moving as quickly as he could to the minivan's sliding door.

He held his Glock as he got down. Pain shot through his leg as he put his full weight on it, but he managed to stand straight. He slid the van door closed behind him. If something went wrong, if gunfire broke out, the van door might provide some protection for those inside. At least that was Max's thinking.

But if things went south, Max wouldn't be able to get back into the van easily. Maybe not at all.

The man with the shotgun was only about fifteen feet away. He was walking steadily towards Max, not varying his pace. He trained his shotgun onto Max's chest.

Max held his Glock down, pointed towards the ground. He didn't want to start things off with the threat of violence. Not unless he needed to.

Maybe what he was doing was crazy. But it seemed like the only solution. They needed to get through this roadblock, and a full out gunfight could have disastrous consequences. Maybe the only option was talking. That was what he was hoping for, at least.

19

JOHN

Somehow John had made it to the shore. He lay there for a full ten minutes on his back, breathing heavily. He was so tired that he didn't even examine his cut right away.

Finally, his muscles aching, John sat up. He lifted his shirt to examine the cut on his side. It was still bleeding, but when he examined it with his fingers, it didn't seem deep enough to be seriously dangerous. At least not immediately. It was the sort of cut that might get infected, though. Not that he had time to worry about that now.

He needed food. And water.

His throat was parched, and he considered drinking from the river. Then he thought better of it.

Then he changed his mind. After all, for all he knew, he might end up walking for miles before he found more water. And here was a ton of it, flowing steadily right past him.

It would have been better if he'd had something to carry it in. Then he could continue on, deciding whether or not to drink the water later, when he became really thirsty.

John dipped his hands into the river and drank. He knew

it was probably polluted with chemicals, not to mention possible pathogens. But the way John figured it, those were long-term problems. He was on the short-term plan, and he knew it. None of it probably mattered. He'd likely be dead by the end of the day.

With nothing but his knife, his clothes soaking wet, John set off. After all, there wasn't anything to do but go on.

When he'd left his apartment, he'd wanted to just do something. He hadn't thought he'd live. He'd just wanted to take action.

In the short time span since leaving, he'd lost and regained that drive too many times to count.

Now he... just didn't know.

So he walked.

Using the sun as his rough guide, he walked northeast.

With each step, he thought of Lawrence bleeding out on the boat. He thought of the farmhouse, the one he knew he'd never arrive at. He thought of his brother, Max, ensconced comfortably in the farmhouse, surrounded by food, water, and guns. He imagined Max having everything planned out perfectly. He imagined Max completely safe from danger.

It was funny that he was thinking about Max after all these years. Either it was because you started to think about your family when you thought you'd die soon. Or it was because Max had always been going on and on about "being prepared."

He was somewhere outside of Southwest Philly. It was south of where the city met the suburbs, some sort of strange industrial area.

There weren't normally many people in this area. There weren't even any sidewalks. It was nothing but factories and warehouses.

John had only been down here once, when he'd gotten lost in a cab on the way to pick up his car from the Parking Authority impound lot. It wasn't the sort of place that you came to unless you had a good reason.

The fact that the area was not residential was working in John's favor now. There wasn't anyone here. Presumably, the workers had gone home.

John walked down the middle of the street. There were some abandoned cars on the side of the road. Some were left with the driver's door open, as if the occupant had fled rapidly.

On a whim, John hopped into one of the cars and tried to start the engine. The keys were in the ignition, after all. But nothing happened. The engine didn't even turn over. Must have been the EMP. Some cars worked. Some didn't. John didn't know why, and he didn't have the energy or interest to speculate on why.

The whole neighborhood was eerily silent. Normally, it would have been filled with the hum of the factories, and the noise of the traffic from a nearby highway.

John walked for what felt like hours. In reality, he didn't know how much time had passed.

Eventually, he had traveled far enough east that the neighborhood had started to change. It was a soft change. Now there were a couple more houses, and even some apartment buildings. There were more trees. He was leaving the city behind.

He didn't notice the sign that marked the official boundary of the city. But he figured he must have missed it, because the farther he walked, the more trees and houses he saw. He'd left the industrial area behind. And with that came the sounds. Sounds of animals. Birds chirped. Squirrels chased each other.

Nature would continue, thought John. The EMP had had a devastating effect on human civilization. But to the animals, nothing had changed. At least not much. Maybe they noticed that the humans were acting differently—John must have been getting exhausted, considering the strange places his mind was going.

His stomach was starting to hurt. He imagined it must have been the water he'd drunk from the Schuylkill River. He tried to ignore the increasing pain, telling himself that it wasn't that bad, or that it was all in his imagination.

John was walking down a normal suburban street. Normal except that no one was out.

The houses had tidy, well-maintained gardens. There were bushes and trimmed hedges. John hadn't been to the suburbs in a long, long time. And this seemed like a strange way to revisit them.

"Hey!" came an unexpected voice. It was male, gruff and weathered.

John didn't know if it was a friendly voice. But he doubted it.

John spun around, looking frantically for the man.

His grip tightened on his kitchen knife.

"Put that down before you hurt yourself."

"Who's there?" said John. "I'm armed..."

"Sure you are," said the voice.

Someone laughed. Someone else. There were multiple people there.

Finally, John saw them. They emerged from a row of dense hedges in front of a normal-looking suburban house. There were three of them. One wore some kind of military uniform. One wore civilian clothes, jeans and a t-shirt. The last wore a police uniform.

John froze. He didn't know what to do. He couldn't take them all on.

But he could try. If he was going to die, at least he could die trying to do something.

To John's surprise, the men stood there and laughed at him, their mouths opening wide, their laughter deep and true, as if they hadn't laughed in ages.

"Seriously, dude, put the knife down."

"We're not going to hurt you."

"Look, we don't even have our guns out."

"Why should I trust you?" said John. He brandished the knife in their direction, even though it was pointless. He saw that each of them had a holstered handgun on their belts.

"Don't tell me you don't recognize me," said the man in the military uniform.

"Recognize you?" said John.

His stomach was causing him great pain, and he was feeling dizzy. He wasn't at his fullest mental faculties, to say the least. Why was this stranger asking him if he recognized him? Why had he called out to John anyway? Was it only to mock him, and watch him while he languished to a death punctuated only by confusion and pain? John's side was hurting, the wound stinging.

"John!" said the man. "It's me, Bill Lastring. From EPR. We worked together, remember? On that Perlman deal?"

"Bill Lastring?" said John, dumbfounded.

He remembered Lastring, a coworker that he'd paired up with for the occasional project.

"But... How? What are you doing in those clothes? I didn't recognize you."

"National Guard," said Bill. "I reported for duty when the EMP hit. The rest is a long, long story."

"I… don't understand." John wasn't sure what it was that he didn't understand. But he didn't know what else to say.

"Come on," said Bill. "I can tell you all about it. But not here."

"Why not?"

"This is a dangerous area," said Bill. "If you want to survive, you've got to get inside."

"And even then, you're not necessarily safe," said one of Bill's companions, the one wearing civilian clothes.

"I…" said John, stuttering, not saying anything at all.

His initial instinct was not to trust these men. Maybe because of what he'd been through. Maybe for another reason altogether. But the fact was that he knew Bill. Not really well. But they'd been casual work buddies. And Bill was a good guy, with a wife and kids.

Deep down, John knew he didn't really have much of a choice. If these guys had wanted to harm him, they'd have already done so. Or they could do so later. John couldn't defend himself against firearms.

While John appeared to be hesitant, his mind was already made up. His grip on his knife was relaxing.

"Come on," said Bill. "Follow us. There's food and water. You can't stay here. The militia makes its rounds."

"The militia?"

But they didn't answer him.

Bill and the two others started walking away, heading between two of the suburban homes.

From somewhere off in the distance, there was a loud, low, rumbling noise. It sounded like a massive truck's engine.

Bill turned around. "They're coming," he said loudly. "Come with us, or…"

John didn't need to be told the rest.

20

MAX

The man with the shotgun had stopped in front of Max. He lowered the shotgun a little. But he still held it purposefully, keeping it pointed at Max's belly. One blast from the gun, and there'd be no saving Max. They weren't equipped to treat stomach wounds, and he'd bleed out right there on the ground under the open sky.

Max continued to study the man's face.

Neither spoke for a full minute.

"We need to get through," said Max finally.

"Who are you?"

"Max, not that that's important anymore."

"What are you doing out here?"

There was deep distrust in the man's voice. But he hadn't yet fired his shotgun. That was a good sign.

If he'd been out to steal the van, he would have acted by now. He wouldn't have hesitated.

Then again, it could be part of some more devious scheme.

Max wasn't yet sure.

"I'm coming from the farmhouse down that way," said Max, gesturing. "Maybe half an hour's drive."

Max was starting to have a feeling that this man was from these parts, that he wasn't some stranger from the city. And there weren't many houses around. Anyone from the area was bound to know which house Max was talking about.

"I inherited the house," said Max. "It's mine. I didn't steal it. I came out here after the EMP, but the area's become overrun. An armed group invaded our home. There's no way we can continue to defend it. So we're heading out of the area. But if we don't pass through, we're never going to make it out."

The man didn't take his eyes off Max. He seemed to be deciding whether Max's story could be true.

"Who are the people in the van?"

"Friends," said Max. "One is a neighbor, one an old friend. The other three were strangers until the EMP. We've been helping each other."

"Why should I believe you?"

"I don't know," said Max.

The more they talked, the more sure Max was becoming that this man wasn't a danger in the way the farmhouse invaders had been. He seemed more like an honest worker from these parts, probably just trying to protect his family. Of course, that didn't make him any less dangerous. Especially not if he ended up deciding Max was a threat.

"I'm going to put my gun down," said Max. "OK?"

Max knew his friends in the minivan would be thinking he was crazy. Hell, they probably already thought he was crazy for doing what he was doing.

He bent down slowly and placed the Glock on the ground, muzzle pointed off to the side.

Max slowly stood straight again, and put his hands in the air.

"We're not a threat," said Max. "Unless we need to be. And I get the feeling the same goes for you."

The man didn't lower his shotgun.

But he spoke.

"We're from here," he said. "Our house is a quarter mile in that direction." He gestured with his head in the direction, making only the slightest movement possible, in order to keep his eyes fixed on Max. His eyes occasionally darted to the minivan. We were fine for the first two weeks. But the last few days, there've been too many people arriving."

"Same thing happened to us," said Max.

"I had to shoot one of them," said the man.

Max didn't say anything.

"I remember your family," said the man. "That is, if you are who you say you are. That house's been in the same family for generations. What's the name of your grandfather?"

"He always went by Hank," said Max.

He saw the man's face relax a little. He knew Max was telling the truth. At least about the farmhouse.

The man nodded ever so slightly. "I didn't know him personally," said the man. "But my dad did."

"We're not looking to hurt you," said Max. "Or take anything from you. All we need is to... to be able to move these logs without getting shot. We'll put them back. I figure you put them here to stop any more cars coming through."

"Yup, trying to limit through traffic."

Max nodded. And he waited for the man's answer.

"We'll let you through," said the man finally. "My name's Miller."

Max breathed a sigh of relief.

"But we're not going to let you get off so easy," said Miller, who hadn't given his first name.

"We don't have many supplies," said Max, cringing at the idea of giving up something that might save their lives later.

Max knew he shouldn't have been surprised that Miller would want something in return. Sure, he'd known Max's family. But this was the apocalypse. Society had collapsed. Everyone, to some extent, had to look out for their own.

The rules had changed.

But to Max's surprise, Miller broke into a smile and finally lowered his shotgun.

"We don't need anything from you," he said. "But I think you could all do with a bit of rest at the very least, before you head on."

Max was speechless. He simply wasn't expecting this.

"You look like you can barely stand up," said Miller. "And I'm going to guess that you all haven't eaten much lately. I don't know where you're headed, but I have the feeling it's a long ways off."

"I don't know," said Max. "We need to push on. The area's going to be overrun soon."

"Well," said Miller. "We've decided to stay. I've had the house set up practically like a bunker for a long, long time. And with this roadblock, well, it'll slow people down a little bit. Those with vehicles, anyway."

Max was hesitating.

It was true, he was so tired he could barely stand up. Half an hour's sleep or so simply wasn't enough, not for well over twenty-four hours.

"You sure your place is safe?" said Max.

"As safe as you're going to get around these parts," said Miller.

It was a tough decision. They needed to get going. But

their chances of survival would be higher if they had some rest, some food. They'd be more likely to make the right decisions. They'd be more likely to react appropriately to danger.

"Penny!" called out Miller, waving over to the other side of the road. Come on out here. We're going to help our new friends out."

From the other side of the road, a woman emerged. She was carrying a shotgun as well. A child, around twelve, followed her.

"Everything OK, Max?" said Georgia, opening the passenger door to the van.

"I think so," said Max. "Excuse me for a minute, will you?" he said to Miller, who gave him a nod.

Max leaned in towards Georgia, and speaking so that everyone in the van could hear, explained the situation.

"They seem trustworthy," said Georgia. "Not that one can ever really know..."

"We trusted each other," said Max. "And I'm glad we did. Not everyone is the enemy."

Georgia nodded. "You're probably right. I hope you're right. But the longer we stay around here, the greater the chances are that we'll get into another gunfight. And that's what we're trying to avoid."

"We can't defend the farmhouse," said Max. "But, frankly, we're going to run into trouble wherever we go. We might as well get some rest while we can. Where we know we're safe."

"I guess we don't really have many other options," said Georgia. "It's a long drive wherever we're going."

"I say we go for it," said Mandy.

"Yeah," said Chad. "And I'm starving."

Everyone agreed, in the end. They got out of the van and

everyone introduced themselves quickly. Meanwhile, they all kept their eyes peeled on the surrounding area. It wasn't exactly the right time for overly cordial introductions.

"We'd better get to the house," said Miller. "You can bring the van."

"How?" said Max.

"Just drive behind me. It doesn't look like there's a path. But trust me, there is. It leads right to our driveway."

"He's been worried about something like this for years," said Penny, Miller's wife. "Everything is set up for the apocalypse. Even the nonexistent trick driveway."

"I'm impressed," said Max.

"Wait 'til you get to the house," said Miller, who started walking off.

Max and everyone else got back into the van. Georgia drove, taking the van slowly over the soft earth.

Miller walked quickly and purposefully ahead of them, Penny and their son trailing him. Husband and wife kept their shotguns at the ready, and from the passenger seat, Max noticed how they constantly scanned the surrounding area.

Finally, they came to the gravel driveway. By removing the portion that connected to the road, Miller had been able to hide the existence of their house more effectively.

Up ahead was Miller's house.

At first glance, it looked like a normal house.

But when they parked and got out, it quickly became clear that there was much more to it.

It was a smallish two story house, with a partially exposed concrete basement. It looked like it had been built in the mid 1970s. Maybe it'd been cheaper to build them that way at that time for some reason.

A ditch had been dug around the exposed concrete walls

of the basement, creating a deep, waterless moat around the house. It was clearly created for protection and defense. It was similar to what Max had envisioned. He'd wanted to dig a ditch around the property of the farmhouse, but this made more sense, now that he saw it.

The effect of the ditch was to create a greater distance between the ground and the second story. It'd make it almost impossible for someone to try to gain access to the second floor by jumping.

"That," said Miller, pointing up to a strange-looking contraption. "Is my pride and joy."

He smiled when he said it. He was proud of it. He'd likely built it himself.

"A drawbridge?" said Max.

"Don't you know it. Come on, I'll show you all how it works. It's the only way into the house. And we'd better not stay out here too long anyway. We'll get everyone inside, and then you and I can come out and put the van in the garage."

He pointed to the garage. It was a squat structure, completely covered with all sorts of foliage, meant to function as camouflage. The disguise had worked well enough that Max hadn't even noticed it. Then again, he was beyond tired.

Miller took them over to the drawbridge, which led to the second floor's door.

"The only door to the basement's been completely sealed off," said Miller. There was true pride showing on his face.

A padlock secured a winch attached to the drawbridge. Miller unlocked it with a key taken from his pocket. This freed the mechanism of the manual winch, and Miller started winding it. The drawbridge slowly lowered.

It was more of a ladder than a real drawbridge. But it served its purpose, preventing easy access to the house.

Miller's wife and child went first, and Miller gestured for everyone else to climb up. There was a small patio at the top, where the drawbridge was attached.

"Want me to help with that?" said Max, standing by the door, as Miller started winding the top-level winch, raising the drawbridge-ladder again.

"I'm good," said Miller. "I like doing it, and you need to rest."

Inside, the house was fairly small. It was only really four rooms, and there was hardly any walking space. Almost every space imaginable had been filled up with canned goods, ammunition, bottles of water, sacks of corn meal, rice, dried beans, all sorts of food stuffs. There were large plastic buckets with labels that held sugar. There was almost everything one could need.

"You've got everything!" said James, excitedly looking around.

"Can I lie down?" said Sadie.

Sadie went right to a small patch of blank floor and lay down, curling up. In a moment, she was asleep, snoring lightly, her hands tucked under her head.

With everyone inside the house, there was hardly any room.

While the house could technically fit all of them, Max knew that it wouldn't work as a long-term solution. Having them all stay there indefinitely, that is. Not that he would ever ask Miller to stay. Miller had done the work to prepare, and Max wasn't going to try to take that away from him. He recognized his own lack of preparation and he was ready to own it.

What was more, Max already had his doubts about

whether Miller's set up would actually work for them. Sure, it was set up better than the farmhouse. But, long term, there were all sorts of problems that could arise, especially if the area was going to become as overrun with stragglers and mercenary types as Max imagined it would.

And, plus, how strong could a padlock really be? A couple hits from an axe and it'd break right off, no matter how well it was made. Miller did seem like the type to take all that into account, and he probably figured that he'd be able to shoot the attacker from above. Sure, shooting from the second floor would provide a tremendous strategic advantage. But would it be enough, day in and day out?

Then again, Max really must have been tired, because he suddenly realized that the padlock was only for when the Millers were away. When they were at home, the ladder would be raised. And when they were away, what good would the padlock do?

Maybe they didn't plan on leaving much. Putting up the roadblocks had been an emergency action, a rare necessity punctuating an otherwise home-bound life.

There were rifles on the walls, and as Miller moved, he revealed a revolver in a holster at his side. The Millers certainly weren't messing around. They were prepared.

As Max should have been. Whatever deficiency possibly existed in Miller's plan, they sure seemed better off than Max's farmhouse group.

Everyone stood around somewhat awkwardly.

"Well," said Miller, clapping his hands together. "Let's get you all something to eat."

He seemed to be enjoying the company.

Mrs. Miller headed into the kitchen, taking her young son in tow, to get something ready for the guests.

"I didn't see a farm on your property," said Max. "Did you work for someone else, or is it hidden?"

"A farmer?" said Miller, smiling. "You took me for a farmer." He started laughing, as if it was the funniest thing in the world. "Can't say I've ever farmed much. I'm a lawyer. Or was, I guess. Legal counsel won't do anyone much good now that there's no law."

"Just the law of the strongest," said Max.

Slowly, everyone was finding a place to sit down, resting their weary bodies. Georgia sat on a bucket, as did James. Chad slumped against a couch, looking like he'd pass out any moment. Mandy's eyes, too, were slowly closing.

"I'm afraid I can't offer you all much more than rice and beans, and some water," said Mrs. Miller, appearing in the doorway to the living room. "Come into the kitchen and serve yourselves."

That really woke everyone up. They practically scrambled to their feet to head into the kitchen, and Miller himself just laughed.

Even though he hadn't yet eaten and rested, Max was feeling more relaxed. It felt good to be here, good to be safe.

But as soon as Max became aware that he was feeling that way, he got that edge of anxiety again. He knew well that it was that edge that had kept him on his toes, and had kept him alive. He couldn't afford to lose it. Not now. Not when there were more and more people coming into the area.

"Come on," Miller said to Max, slapping him on the back. "Let's get that minivan into the garage. You can all spend the night here, if you can find space on the floor, that is." He laughed, taking pleasure in the quantity of his preparations.

The others were already eating, practically drinking down their bowls of rice and beans.

Max forwent food to follow Miller back outside, where they went through the complicated business of the winch and the lowering of the ladder again.

"How'd you come up with this whole idea?" said Max, gesturing to the ladder. He wanted to ask Miller if he thought it would really help him protect his family. Max wasn't exactly the type to not say what he meant, but he was staying in the man's home, and eating his food. There were some lines of politeness that he wouldn't cross, even as civilization crashed down around them.

"The drawbridge?" said Miller, smiling proudly. "Thought of it all myself."

Max nodded, as he looked out towards the trees in the distance.

The two stood together, side by side, looking out across the huge, overgrown yard toward the tall trees.

"You know," said Miller. "Your grandfather helped my dad out a lot once. I don't know the details or anything. I think it was something like a big financial loan, but I'm not sure."

"Yeah?"

"Just glad I can repay the favor, is all."

"We appreciate it," said Max. "We're dead tired."

"I can tell."

Suddenly, Max saw something. It was movement between the trees. Someone was out there, wearing a bright red shirt.

His first thought wasn't, "shit, not again. I can't deal with this." No, somehow Max's mind went right to the practical, right to what had to be done.

"You see that?" said Max, pointing.

Whoever was out there, they were too far away to hear Max.

"Shit," muttered Miller. "Not again. I don't want to have to shoot anyone else."

"You might have to," said Max.

"Don't get me wrong. I will," said Miller, wincing as he said it. "I just..."

"I know," said Max. "No one likes to... unless they're sick."

"Maybe they'll just move on through," said Miller. "There's no sign yet that they'll attack us."

"I hope so," said Max.

The figure in the red shirt was clearer now, but still very far away. Whoever it was, they weren't even remotely a threat yet.

But as Max continued to watch, he saw more figures moving through the trees.

They emerged from the trees, moving as a pack, coming straight towards Miller's home. It was getting clearer that they were after the house, and whatever it contained, whoever they were.

"Shit," said Miller. "Shit, shit, shit."

"We had three guys attack us," said Max. "They took the farmhouse. We almost didn't make it..."

"We'll be fine," said Miller.

"We had six people with guns," said Max.

"We'll be fine," said Miller. "Don't you worry. I'm a good shot, and so is my wife. Even my son... But he's never shot anyone..."

"We'll help," said Max. "You're letting us stay in your home."

Miller turned to him and shook his head. "No," he said. "I'm not going to let someone else fight my fights for me."

"We're talking about the safety of your family," said Max. "It's even more than that... we're talking about the *lives* of your wife, and your son, not to mention your own."

"We'll be fine," said Miller. "But you'd all better leave. You don't want to get mixed up in this. Maybe you had the right idea leaving the area. We're too close to the cities. Too many people are coming, looking for a way out."

"This is crazy," said Max. "You'd do better with six extra guns."

But Max could tell that he wouldn't change Miller's mind. It showed in his face, and Max knew that Miller wasn't the sort of person who was going to put others at risk, even if it meant risking his own family.

Max didn't agree with the decision, but there wasn't anything he could do about it. Plus, he didn't want to admit it to himself, but he and the others would be better off the sooner they could get away from this mess.

"Come with us," said Max, trying one more time. "You've got a car or truck, right?"

Miller nodded. "A truck."

"Great, then follow us on out of here. We could use a guy like you with us on the road, someone who knows what he's doing."

"We've got all our supplies," said Miller. "We can't take it all..."

"You could take a lot of it," said Max. "You've got six sets of hands that can help you load it all quickly."

Miller shook his head adamantly. "I'm not leaving my home," he said. "I just can't do that."

Max finally knew there was nothing more to say. There was no good words could do. He didn't know if the Millers would make it through the rest of the day alive. But it wasn't his battle.

"Mandy, Georgia!" called out Max, moving closer to the home.

"What is it?" came Mandy's sleepy voice as she poked her head out the window. She looked like she'd just been woken up. Her eyes were blurry, and her hair was messy and undone, hanging around her face. It was a strange time for such a thought, but Max was suddenly struck again with her beauty. The thought distracted him, and it took him a moment to speak.

"We're leaving," he called out.

"What?"

"We're leaving. Now!" Max waved his arms urgently. "Get everyone. Get everything."

There wasn't time to wait around. They needed to leave as fast as possible.

"If you head that way," said Miller, pointing. "You can drive across the property for a quarter of a mile and get around both roadblocks we set up."

Mad nodded. "Good luck."

"You too."

Max was already limping towards the van, and Miller was already up his drawbridge-ladder.

Max had the minivan started by the time the first of his group was down the ladder. He rolled down the automatic window on the passenger's side and yelled at them to hurry up and get in.

They all moved sleepily and slowly, until they saw the figures off in the distance. The figures were staying still, possibly waiting until the right moment to move in and attack. If that was what they were going to do. If the Millers were lucky, nothing would happen at all.

"Why aren't we staying to help?" said Chad, to Max's pleasant surprise, as he got in the car.

"I offered," was all Max said.

"They should come with us," said Mandy, getting into the seat behind Max.

"He won't," said Max.

"Are you OK to drive, Max?" said Georgia.

"Yeah," was all Max said.

He had the van moving before the last door was closed. He used the rear view mirror to check to see that everyone was there.

Maybe it was because of his exhaustion, or the surreal nature of the situation, but these thoughts kept popping into Max's head, thoughts that weren't directly related to the practical. The last one had been about Mandy's beauty. This one was about how when the EMP had first struck, Max had been concerned about one person and one person only—himself. Himself, and no one else. Now he was going so far as to check to make sure everyone was in the van. He was concerned for the lives of people he hadn't even met until two weeks ago. He felt responsible for them, and he didn't even know why. Maybe it gave him a purpose. Maybe it gave him something to fight for.

The van was moving slowly across the bumpy road.

Max adjusted the mirror again, trying to see out the back. But he couldn't see the men, not from this angle.

"Can anyone see them?"

"Nope," said Chad. "We're too far away. Last I saw, they were just standing there."

"I hope they don't hurt the Millers," said Sadie. "They're so nice."

"Mrs. Miller gave us supplies on the way out," said James. "She gave us a big bag of rice, and even some beef jerky."

"Just don't eat it all yourself, James," said Sadie. "And she gave us water bottles, too."

That was good, that they had more food and water. But Max's mind was on the Millers' imminent danger.

Miller was sure to be inside by now, his drawbridge-ladder hoisted. He'd have his gun in his hand, and so would his wife. Maybe his son, too.

But Max couldn't think about them now.

"I can't believe they're staying," said Mandy.

"They've made their decision," said Georgia.

Finally, they made it to the road, emerging just past the second roadblock, which was a pile of tree stumps that Miller must have dragged over with his truck earlier in the day, before felling those trees.

The minivan moved smoothly on the pavement. Max pressed down on the accelerator, and the van started to gather speed.

"Max!" cried out someone.

In front of them, on the road, was a figure. There wasn't enough time to register who they were.

The figure was dashing off to the road's shoulder, a handgun raised.

A shot rang out. The sound of shattering glass.

Max acted without thinking. He swung the wheel, urging the van directly towards the figure.

21

JOHN

The four of them were sitting in a dark, unfurnished basement. The only illumination came from the sunlight that crept through the cracks of the small, boarded up windows.

Bill's two companions had introduced themselves, but John had already forgotten their names.

They'd given John a full water bottle, which he'd drained in almost a single gulp. And they'd handed him a loaf of stale sliced bread. It was cheap supermarket bread, the kind of stuff that John would have turned his nose up at just a little more than two week ago. But he ate it greedily, devouring the whole loaf in record time.

"So I don't get it," said John. "The whole Main Line area has been taken over by some militia?"

"Shhh, remember to whisper."

"Sorry," whispered John.

"If they find us, we're screwed," whispered Bill. "Trust me, they're brutal. You wouldn't believe the things they've done... the things I've seen...."

Bill had probably saved John's life, taking him down to

this basement. It was evidently a place they'd hidden out in before, since Bill had known exactly which window was unlocked. Maybe he'd left it that way himself.

Bill hadn't mentioned his family at all, and John didn't want to ask. He had a feeling that something horrible had happened to them, and he didn't want to cause Bill any pain by asking about it. At least that was what he was telling himself. Really, he thought of himself nothing more than a coward for not even asking.

"To answer your question," said one of the men, speaking in low tones. "The military and police had control of the area. From what you're saying, it sounds like they only lasted a short while in Philly."

"Yeah," said John, who didn't want to say anything more about the horrors in the city. Those screams he'd heard would be featured in his nightmares and waking thoughts for the rest of his life, which for all he knew wasn't going to be much longer.

"They lasted about a week out here," continued the man. In the darkness, John couldn't tell if he was the one wearing civilian clothes or the police uniform. "But without communication, everything fell apart quickly."

"Too quickly," interjected Bill.

The other one grunted in acknowledgment.

"That's the thing I don't understand about any of this," said John. "It was like... first there were riots. I mean, there've been riots before, ugly ones. And there's almost always looting when the power is out for a couple days... But things got crazy too quickly... Too quickly..."

"We've talked it to death already," said Bill. "Basically, it doesn't make any sense unless you consider that it's just what we are."

"What do you mean?" said John. He was feeling better

now, with the bread in his stomach, refilling his glycogen stores slowly, and his thirst quenched.

"We were all brought up believing that we're all civilized humans," said Bill. "We were brought up believing that all those crazy, horrible things in history were from a long, long time ago, and that we've progressed past that. They told us in school how the early humans fought brutal tribal wars, slaughtering each other, how they ate each other, etc. But we always considered our ancestors something completely different from ourselves. We're the modern humans. But in reality, we're nothing more than cavemen dressed in suits."

John laughed, to his own surprise. "That's what they used to say about us investment guys. Or something like that. That we're sharks in suits, basically. Savage interior, well-dressed exterior."

"Exactly," said Bill. "And once the suits and modern society suddenly drop away, what's left? Nothing but the primitive savage who's willing to do anything for his own survival."

"Or what he considers necessary for his own survival," said John. "I've seen things that made no sense. Things that didn't benefit anyone."

"Part of the package," said Bill.

"So what are you guys doing hiding out here?" said John. He couldn't exactly put the pieces together of what was going on.

"We're deserters, basically," said Bill. "I didn't like what was going."

"To put it lightly."

"We call the organization that's formed the militia, but it doesn't really have anything to do with the military. Not the military we once had. And certainly not the police force."

"They were executing people," said Bill. "Like some kind of demented martial law in effect. It was horrible."

John wondered if that was how Bill had lost his wife and child. But still, he didn't dare ask. And he hated himself for not asking.

"So I imagine they're not so happy about that, about you deserting?" said John.

"No," said Bill, shaking his head.

"They want total control of the area," said the other. "And they're vicious. They'll do whatever it takes. Trust me, whatever."

"It sounds chaotic," said John.

"Sort of. It's actually pretty organized. Considering that there's no real means of communication. They've started using runners, though, to send messages through to the other leaders."

"And what's the goal of all this?" said John.

"Control? Power? Who knows. The people who lead the militia—maybe they were frustrated with their old lives. Maybe they were always on the bottom of the hierarchy. Now they've clawed their way to the top. And they want to punish the others."

"There's also the practical aspect of it all. Those at the top get the most food. The water, and the booze."

"I can't imagine that's going to last long," said John. "Not without any food being shipped here."

"And don't forget most of the farms in the US are heavily automated," said Bill. "Don't think that those farms out in the Midwest are going to be able to grow corn and wheat like before. Maybe eventually. But not for a long while. And still the food won't get here."

"Has the militia started on plans to produce here in the suburbs?" said John.

"Not from what we can tell," said Bill. "The whole thing is bound to collapse when the food that's available here runs out. But there's quite a bit of it, if you consider all the stores that are packed full, and all the food in people's houses. And it's not like it's being divided up equally. Far from it. Those at the top of the hierarchy get the most. They're the only ones with full stomachs."

"And what about you guys?" said John. "Are you like the resistance or something?"

Bill and the others laughed.

"I suppose so," said Bill. "Although I don't think we've ever actually said that."

"And what are your plans?" said John.

"To get out," said Bill.

"We can't take them all on. There's just no way. We've been hiding out in basements and stuff for the last few days. But we won't last long here."

There was silence for a moment in the dark basement.

"You want to come with us?" said Bill.

"Yeah," said John, without hesitating, without even asking where they were going. "When are we leaving?"

"Tonight," said Bill.

The four of them fell into silence for a while longer. Each of them seemed to be lost in their own thoughts.

John tried to think of the journey ahead, and what it would entail. But he knew in his heart that there was simply no way he could predict the coming dangers and trials. He'd already been through so much. His mind and body weren't ready for more. But there was no other option. He had to keep going.

The light outside was starting to grow dim as the sun fell lower in the sky. It was late afternoon and it would be dusk soon.

The rumbling truck in the distance hadn't passed down this street, or they would have heard it for sure. There were no sounds outdoors except the chirping of the birds.

Bill had a small medical kit and he put something on John's cut. It stung, but John hardly even paid attention to it. There was so much to think about, and so much to avoid thinking about, that he'd completely forgotten about the cut, not to mention his stomach problems. Those were simply the least of his worries.

Clear plastic tubs were stacked along one wall of the basement. They were full of children's toys, stuffed animals, train tracks, and toy soldiers. Next to the tubs, there was a child's mountain bike.

This had been someone's house. A family's house. Children had lived here and played here. Maybe they'd been old enough to go to school. The parents had gone to work, gone to the grocery store, cooked dinner, watched movies, and made love. Whole lives had been lived in this house.

And now there was nothing left but their possessions, hastily abandoned. What had happened to the family here? What had happened to the children? Had the parents waited like John had, until something awful had happened? Or had the parents hastily packed their children and some essentials into the car, only to get stuck on the roads somewhere? Had they all died on some overcrowded, jam-packed highway? Had their car even started? There was no way to know. And it wasn't fun to think about.

Suddenly, a sound rang out.

It was someone knocking on the door. Knocking loudly.

Whoever it was, they knocked incessantly. Constantly.

John hadn't heard anyone approaching. He hadn't heard any vehicles.

John froze.

In the dim light, he saw Bill and the others reaching for their guns, which they had laid on the floor, or against the walls.

Bill and the others rose slowly to their feet, making gestures at each other.

John rose too, but he didn't know what to do. He didn't have a gun. And no one handed him one. In fact, no one even looked at him. And why should they? It wasn't their job to protect him. It was everyone for themselves.

John searched blindly with his hand for his knife on the ground. He found it, and his hand formed a fist around its handle once again. It was comforting having something in his hand, even if he knew it wouldn't do much good against a gun. No good at all, really.

But he clutched it anyway.

John didn't dare to speak. But he desperately wanted to ask what to do. He wanted some direction. He wanted a plan to follow, something concrete. But he knew that was a ridiculous wish. There were no plans. No certainty. No safety.

Glass shattered on the first floor, the sound coming down loudly to the basement.

Whoever was up there, they'd just broken a window. Soon, they'd be inside the house.

22

MANDY

The bullet had pierced the glass of the passenger window and lodged itself in Max's headrest. No one was hit. But that was only pure luck. Maybe they wouldn't be so lucky next time. And there was sure to be a next time. There always was. There was no rest for them, and Mandy wondered if there ever would be.

The right portion of the front bumper had smashed into the person on the side of the road. The body had crumpled underneath the minivan, and they'd felt the sickening bump as the van drove right over the body.

No one looked behind them. No one spoke. But Sadie screamed, and then fell silent.

They had all been through so much that, strangely, getting shot and running over a stranger wasn't really that big of a deal. What a horrible reality they were living in, thought Mandy.

Looking straight ahead, Max was driving them quickly down the highway, heading west, towards Ohio.

The sky was darkening. The evening was approaching. Soon they'd be facing the night, and who knew what terrible dangers awaited them out on the open road. Mandy couldn't help but think about how they were even less prepared than they'd been two weeks ago. When she and Max had left the suburbs, they'd had maps. They'd had a plan. They knew where they were going, and they thought they'd be safe there.

Now, their haven had become dangerous, and their eventual fate was a mystery.

Mandy's mind turned to the Millers and what awaited them. Maybe they were fighting for their lives right in this moment. Maybe the battle had happened quickly, and the Millers had triumphed. Or maybe the Millers had become nothing but bodies lying on the floor, soon to be pushed aside and forgotten. Or maybe nothing had happened at all, the strangers retreating back into the trees, leaving the Millers to live and fight another day.

Mandy looked over at Sadie and James, in the seats next to her. They were both fast asleep. Sadie rested her head on James's shoulder. Mandy felt a pang in her chest. They were too young to be going through this. They deserved to be living the normal lives of teenagers. They deserved to have the rest of their lives stretched out in front of them, open books that they could do with what they wished.

"Where are we going?" said Mandy, tapping Max on the shoulder. She sat in the seat directly behind him.

"West," said Max. His voice was tired, and it cracked a little as he spoke.

"We need a plan," said Mandy.

"I know," said Max. "But we also need to get out of this area before something else happens."

"You're too tired," said Mandy. "I can hear it in your voice. Let me drive."

"I'm fine," said Max.

"No, you're not. We all need to rest while we can. Who knows what's going to happen next. And it'd be better for us all if you're well rested."

Chad had joined James and Sadie in falling asleep, and Georgia wasn't far behind. In the passenger's seat, Mandy could see that her head kept bobbing back and forth as she jerked herself awake every couple minutes. She was probably too worried about her kids to let herself fully fall asleep just yet.

"You're right," Max finally admitted. "I'll pull over soon."

Max switched the headlights off and continued to drive for another ten minutes in the dusky darkness. He drove more slowly, since there was just enough light to drive by.

Mandy knew that he didn't want headlights blazing into the woods, alerting anyone who could be nearby of their presence.

Finally, Max pulled off to the side of the road. She noticed that he kept all four wheels on the pavement, probably in case they needed to make a quick get away. After all, who knew where they were or what dangers awaited them here. The road didn't look much different than it had back by the farmhouse. It was tree lined and peaceful looking. But looks could be deceptive.

"What's going on?" said Sadie, waking up, her voice full of sleep.

"It's OK, Sadie," said Mandy. "I'm going to drive for a while. We're just changing drivers."

"Don't forget the flowers," said Sadie, speaking as if she was in a dream. She fell back asleep immediately. James and Chad slumbered on, dead to the world. It was a testament to how much they'd all pushed themselves. There was always a limit, and they'd all reached it. The human body was capable of incredible feats, but the rules of biology and physics still applied, no matter what. It was lucky they'd all been able to last as long as they had.

Max had his gun in his hand when he stepped out of the car.

Mandy had to navigate her way through James's and Sadie's legs to get out through the sliding side door.

"You sure you're OK to drive?" said Max, approaching her in the near-darkness.

He stood close to her, and she could viscerally feel his presence near her. She was acutely aware of how close his body was to hers.

Mandy felt a pain in her heart. If things had been different, if the EMP had never happened, maybe something could have happened between Max and her. Sure, they'd never known each other, even as neighbors. But sooner or later, maybe they would have run into each other. Maybe some situation would have forced them to get to know each other. Like a normal power outage, a localized one that lasted only a few hours, forcing Mandy to head next door to see if Max had some candles. A romance could have easily developed between them, and who knew what it could have possibly become.

Countless lives had already been lost. But there were other, subtler things, that had been lost as well. Things and feelings that had been cruelly snuffed out.

"I'm fine," Mandy finally said. "And you need to sleep."

Mad nodded. She could see the exhaustion in his eyes, even in the dim light.

"What are we going to do?" said Mandy. "Are we going to just keep driving? Or are we going to camp somewhere?"

"I think we'd better get as far away as possible," said Max. "We can take shifts driving. There's no reason to camp. Not now. It just makes us more vulnerable."

"I guess you're right," said Mandy. "There hasn't been a single other car on the road. I wonder why."

"Who knows," said Max.

"I guess it's better not to worry about these things too much."

"Well," said Max. "It'd be helpful if we knew more about what's going on. That's what's so hard about this. It's hard to make a plan without information."

"And there's no way to get that information."

Max shook his head, agreeing with her.

"What about gas?" said Mandy. "We can't just drive forever. How much gas do we have?"

"A little more than half a tank," said Max.

"We've already used that much?"

"It's an older vehicle," said Max. "And we're dragging a lot of weight along with us."

"So how do we get more gas?"

Max shrugged. "We'll have to get it somewhere," he said. "Or else we're back to walking. We can siphon it, provided we find another car. Maybe we'll get lucky and hit a gas station."

"You think the gas station would still work?"

"Probably not," said Max. "But it's worth a try."

"Maybe we'd be better off just walking," said Mandy.

"Why?"

"I feel like we're out in the open on the road," said Mandy. "Sooner or later we're bound to run into trouble. A roadblock, or a town. Or another car. Who knows. Anything could happen. If we were walking, we could cut through the woods, take the routes no one would hit, where there won't be anybody."

"Yeah," said Max. "I was thinking along the same lines. But the problem is that we don't have maps of anywhere but

Pennsylvania. And I think we're better off driving out of here. It'll take us forever to walk across the whole state. And the faster we're out of here, the better."

"You think things will be any different in Ohio?"

"I doubt it," said Max. "It's pretty populated. It'd be a little better in Indiana. I won't rest easy until we hit Nebraska or Wyoming, though. And that's a long, long way to go."

"You think we'll make it that far?"

"I don't know," said Max.

"Maybe we can find some out of the way place in Ohio," said Mandy. "Head to the middle of some state park or something."

"We might have to," said Max. "The only thing to do right now is to keep going."

They stood in silence for a moment, facing each other, their bodies close but not touching. Before, there would have been the possibility that they'd kiss. And Mandy felt that possibility viscerally, in her body.

But nothing happened. Neither of them moved. There were too many uncertainties. Too much danger.

"I'm worried about you, Max," said Mandy, finally.

"I'm fine," said Max.

"Are you taking your antibiotics for your wound?"

"As often as I can," said Max. "Don't worry about me."

"I do, though. You should be resting."

"It's not like that's really an option."

"I know, but..." Mandy didn't have anything to add. It was the start of a sentence that went nowhere. Given their uncertain future, such a sentence somehow felt appropriate.

"I wish we had some painkillers for you. It'd help your leg."

"They'd just cloud my thinking," said Max. "The pain keeps me sharp."

Mandy remembered how Max had insisted on giving Chad's Vicodin to the dying man. It had only been a couple weeks ago, but it felt almost like a lifetime ago. So much happened. And it wasn't like their story was over. Not yet. Not for a long while.

"We'd better get going," said Mandy, moving away from Max.

They both got into the van.

Max was already asleep by the time Mandy put the van into drive.

She was the only one awake as the evening became night, and she drove silently, lost in her own thoughts.

She kept her eye on the gas gauge, which seemed to be dropping towards empty too fast. Maybe it was just her imagination. She hoped it was just her imagination.

For much of the way, there were only trees that lined the road. But later on, there was the occasional old house that sat close to the road. Of course, no lights shone from them. Mandy found herself wondering whether they were inhabited or not. Any of those houses looked like a nice, comfortable place where they could all spend the night. But it was too much of a risk. Most likely, each of the houses contained a fearful family, with a father or mother who was doing their best to stay awake, a gun on the bedside table.

Mandy, Max, and the others weren't the sort of people who'd take something just because they could. They weren't going to rob innocent people. They were concerned with defending themselves. Not hurting others.

At about 9 o'clock, Mandy saw headlights in the distance, down the road towards them.

She became so nervous that she found herself holding

her breath. So much could happen. So much could go wrong. Who knew who was in the car, or what their intentions were. They could be people just like Max and Mandy and the others. Or they could be like the people who'd invaded the farmhouse, looking to take what they wanted without a care for who they hurt. They could even be the sorts of people who relished the opportunity to hurt and destroy, the sorts who had been waiting their whole lives for an opportunity like this, when law and order fell to the way side. Mandy shuddered as she remembered those men who'd broken into her apartment. It had happened so quickly after the EMP that it was almost hard to believe. But it had happened. Mandy had been there and felt their hands on her and seen the malice in their eyes.

Mandy didn't know what to do. She kept driving, heading right towards the headlights.

There was a chance that the oncoming car would swerve to block them. And there was a chance that they'd just pass each other on the road, like two normal cars on any normal day in America.

Mandy didn't know why, but she didn't wake anyone up. She let them sleep.

She was hoping for the best. She was hoping nothing would happen.

23

JOHN

There were footsteps upstairs. The floorboards above them creaked and groaned as people walked and stomped around.

At first, John had been hoping it'd just been one person up there. One person who'd broken the window and entered the house. One person who was a threat.

Instead, it sounded like many.

Whoever they were, they weren't speaking. That probably meant they knew, or suspected, that others were in the house. That wasn't good.

Maybe they just wouldn't come down into the basement.

But John knew that was too much to hope for. He knew enough by now to know that things simply didn't go the way he'd hope. Usually, they went the worst way possible.

John watched as Bill and the others moved themselves against the wall. They pointed their guns at the end of the staircase.

John didn't know what to do. He had no military training, and he knew his knife would be no good. Which was good. Truthfully, he was terrified of the thought of *having* to use it.

He moved against the wall himself, staying behind Bill. The two others were against the other wall. None of them moved.

The door above them opened. It creaked loudly.

But maybe they still wouldn't come down. Maybe they were just opening the door to see if it was a closet or something. Maybe they'd lose interest when they saw that it led to a basement.

Then again, whoever they were, they were almost certainly looking for provisions. And everyone knew that tons of useful things were often kept in basements.

John's heart was pounding in his chest. Adrenaline was coursing through him. He felt tense and wired. And cold with fear. He tried to keep his breathing under control. He felt like he was making far too much noise just breathing.

Footsteps on the stairs.

Heavy footsteps.

Someone was descending.

Each stair creaked. John's heart leaped with each step.

It was brutal, the waiting.

He wished it could just all be over. No matter what the end, surely it'd be better than this. The suspense alone might kill him.

When the person was about halfway down the stairs, at least as far as John could tell, counting the steps in his head and doing guesswork, they switched on a bright flashlight. The beam hit the wall opposite the stairs. It was a concentrated beam, but it cast diffuse light across the basement. Dust particles seemed to hang in the air, glowing with light.

Everything felt still as the unknown person descended.

Just get it over with, said John over and over to himself in his head.

John saw the foot first. Wearing a heavy military-style boot, lots of laces, camo fatigues stuffed into the top of the boot.

Bill's companion, the man in the civilian clothes, shot first.

The sound was defending, blasting John's eardrums. It rang out through the basement, echoing horribly.

John crouched down in fear, acting instinctually, automatically, covering his head with his hands. Just a coward, he thought to himself, the thoughts ringing painfully through his head, almost as bad as the gunfire. Nothing more than a damn coward.

Another shot. A series of shots.

Muzzle flashes lit up the room. The flashlight dropped, rolling to the floor. Its clatter couldn't even be heard over the gunfire.

John didn't know what was happening. It was too much. Too fast.

More footsteps, thudding around upstairs. Yelling. Shouted commands. All guttural and intense.

"Tim's down," shouted someone, either Bill or the other guy.

John looked up. The civilian-clothed companion was down on the ground, bleeding profusely.

There was another body on the ground. It was a woman wearing military camo. She'd fallen headfirst down the last few steps, out over the open side of the stairwell. Her long braided hair ran down her back, out of a green military-style baseball cap. She lay face down, her gun underneath her body. One of her boots was still resting on a stair.

"They're not going to come down," said Bill, in hurried, hushed tones.

He was speaking mostly to the cop. Not to John. He knew John wasn't going to be any good. He knew John was just dead weight, a worthless goner, no matter what.

There was no way out of this. And John knew he'd be the next to die. Maybe he deserved it. He wasn't doing anyone any good. Not even himself.

"Yeah," said the cop. John still didn't know his name, and they were going to die together. "There's no reason to. They'll just wait for us to come up."

"Or drop a grenade down here," said Bill.

There was no discussion of the people upstairs simply leaving. But John already knew that that simply wasn't going to happen.

"The window," muttered Bill, gesturing with his head towards one of the small windows.

"Looks small."

"We could get through it."

"They're sure to be outside, though. Waiting."

"What do we do?"

"I've got no idea."

"Shit."

There was shouting upstairs.

"Throw it!"

Something clattered down the stairs. Something heavy and dense.

John saw it. It was a grenade. It lay on the dusty concrete floor. Time seemed to stand still for a moment.

But there wasn't time to move.

It exploded.

The shock wave hit them. John's eardrums rang from the sound of the explosion.

Bill's heavy body hit him, knocking him over. John was on the ground, underneath Bill.

John knew he should have felt something. Some shrapnel piercing him. He should have felt pain. But he felt nothing except for Bill's heaviness weighing down on him. It was hard for him to breathe, and his eardrums sang with pain.

With the ringing in his ears, it was hard to tell, but John guessed that silence followed the grenade.

There were thumping footsteps. Someone was headed down the stairs.

"Bill!" said John, whispering loudly. "Bill!"

But he already knew there'd be no response. Bill didn't move. He wasn't breathing.

John didn't know why, and he didn't know how, but somehow he had the strength to go on. The strength to at least try.

It took all his strength to push Bill off of him.

Bill's dead weight finally fell to the side, making a sickening noise as it slumped down onto the concrete. The sound of cold death, boring, mundane, and terrifying.

Bill's back was bloodied with shrapnel wounds.

The cop was down on the ground, not moving. He was lying face up, his chest and face torn up by shrapnel. There wasn't any hope for him.

John felt dizzy and weak. He still had his knife. His only thought was that somehow he could get out through the window. Not that he *could* but that he needed to try.

A man wearing fatigues and a t-shirt jumped down the last few steps. His boots landed heavily on the concrete floor. The light was dim, but John could still see him. The dead woman's flashlight lay on the ground, shining its concentrated beam at the opposite wall, offering only diffuse light to the surroundings.

The man saw John instantly.

He raised his handgun, pointing it at John's head.

It was over. It was finally over.

There was nothing he could do.

A small bit of relief washed over John.

Finally.

The man pulled the trigger. John saw it all happen almost in slow motion.

He knew he'd be dead in an instant.

But nothing happened.

The gun had jammed.

John looked up, finally meeting the man's gaze. He looked him dead in the eyes. And he saw fear.

24

GEORGIA

Georgia had tried to stay awake. After all, she'd needed to protect James and Sadie. And the rest of the group needed her too. But she'd pushed herself past her limits, and finally fallen asleep in the van's passenger seat.

"Did anything happen?" said Georgia, finally opening her eyes.

The first thing she did was turn around to look at James and Sadie. They were sound asleep.

The night was dark. It was only because of the headlights that she could see the road stretching out in front of the minivan. The trees on the road side looked eerie in the off-white glow of the headlights.

"Nothing," said Mandy, sounding tired herself.

"There weren't any other cars?"

"Well, I saw one," said Mandy. "I was really worried. I saw the headlights coming towards us, and I almost had a heart attack."

"You should have woken us up," said Georgia.

"Nothing happened," said Mandy. "They just drove right on by."

"Something could have happened," said Georgia.

"I guess you're right. So what's the plan?"

"Well, for one thing, it's my turn to drive. You need to get some sleep."

Mandy slowed the van down, and she and Georgia switched places.

Max stirred in the backseat. "I'm not going to sleep anymore," he said. "I'll take the passenger seat. Mandy, you can sleep in the back with the others."

It felt strange to be behind the wheel of the minivan. This was the sort of vehicle that Georgia had always hated, even though she was a mother herself and could understand its practicality. Georgia had always preferred trucks.

Georgia had to admit that the minivan was serving them well now. A truck wouldn't have fit all of them.

And the minivan ran without problems. At least so far. The engine hummed quietly. The accelerator felt smooth, and there didn't seem to be any problems with the automatic transmission.

"Mandy saw someone else on the road," said Georgia. "Another car."

"She should have woken us up," said Max.

"That's what I told her."

Mandy was already fast sleep behind them, her soft snores barely audible.

Max handed Georgia a bottle of water from the Millers, as well as a bag of beef jerky. She took a bite of the tough home-made beef jerky and felt a little stronger almost instantly. It was good beef jerky, made with a mixture of just the right spices. It was too bad they didn't have more food like that. Who knew how much they could withstand with good food in their stomachs. Then again, they'd already withstood a lot.

Soon enough, Georgia would be able to hunt again, and they wouldn't have to worry so much about food. All she needed was a place where she wasn't likely to get ambushed. Unfortunately, a place like that was proving hard to find. Harder than they'd thought.

"So what's the plan, Max?" she asked.

"Well," said Max, leaning over to get a better look at the gas gauge. "We're going to need gas soon. At least by dawn, at the rate we're burning through fuel."

"You think we'll be able to get it?"

"I hope so. It's either that or get another vehicle."

"One that can fit us all?"

"Two cars, if we need to," said Max. "One would be better."

"How are we going to get gas? Will the gas stations work?"

"I doubt it," said Max. "The pumps are powered by electricity. The EMP will have fried everything."

"I remember reading that some gas stations had generators," said Georgia. "That way, they'd keep working during a natural disaster."

"Right," said Max. "I think in parts of Florida, where they kept getting hit with hurricanes, some gas stations had generators installed. As far as I know, they've never done the same thing in Pennsylvania. Not that it would do us much good anyway. The generators will have been fried as well."

"Shit," said Georgia.

"Shit is right," said Max. "And it's not like we can just suck the gas out of there. On the internet, people always used to talk about siphoning gas from a gas station with a hose."

"That wouldn't work," said Georgia. She had enough common sense to understand why.

"Right," said Max. "It works with gravity. So if the tank is in the ground, the gas isn't going to magically travel up the tube against the force of gravity."

"So gas stations are out?" said Georgia.

"I guess," said Max. "Unless we can come up with some physics-defying brilliant plan. But for now, I think we'd better focus on finding another car."

"An abandoned one?"

"Preferably not a car with an occupant," said Max. "But we're desperate. I'm not going to go around checking to see if anyone still needs the car or not. Call it stealing. Or whatever you want. But that's what we're going to have to do. If we want to get out of here, that is."

"I don't think Mandy's going to be happy about that."

"She's going to have to deal with it," said Max.

They drove in silence for a while, heading through the dark night. There were no other cars on the road.

"How's the leg?" said Georgia.

"Fine," said Max. He fished in his pocket for his bottle of antibiotics, and shook a pill out into his hand. He swallowed it without water.

"I don't get it," said Georgia. "There were so many people in our area. But I don't see any cars out here. You'd think people would be traveling by car."

"I think what happened," said Max, "is that most people are coming from the cities and the dense suburbs. The roads must have become impassable shortly after we made it out. Traffic jams, military blockades, accidents... a thousand things could have prevented the use of the roads. This is a small two lane road that heads east and west. We're not seeing a lot of cars on it because most of the cars are stuck in the cities. And most of the people who live out here are probably staying. They're getting ready to defend their homes. They're more likely to be prepared for an event like this than the people in the cities. It's a mindset kind of thing."

"Unfortunately," said Georgia, "that's going to mean that we're less likely to find a car out here. If most of them are stuck in the cities and 'burbs."

"We'll find one," said Max. "There are still cars out here."

"We'd better find one soon," said Georgia. "Or else we're not going to be able to make it much farther. Look at the gas gauge."

"I know," said Max.

"Too bad we don't have any gas cans with us," said Georgia.

"I was thinking about that," said Max. "I think we might be able to use the plastic sack meant for extra water."

"I guess that could work. But we might get into a situation where we need to store extra water."

"We'll have to go thirsty," said Max.

"It's one of the basic life necessities," said Georgia. "It's the most essential thing..."

"Getting out is the most essential thing," said Max. "At least for now. It's a risk. And it's one we might have to take."

Up ahead, in the dark night, there was a house in the distance. The clouds had parted, and the moonlight shone down on the lone house.

"Look," said Georgia. "I think that's a car out front."

"It is," said Max, peering through the windshield. "Now's our chance."

Georgia slowed the van down, giving them a chance to figure out what to do.

"You sure you want to do this?" said Georgia. "It's someone's gas, after all."

"We don't have any choice," said Max.

"Maybe we could head off into the woods somewhere," said Georgia. "Maybe we'll be able to get out of the way…"

"You know that's not going to work, Georgia," said Max. "Do you want your kids to be safe? Or do you want to stay awake every night in the woods, wondering if someone will find us that night or the next?"

Max wasn't the type to use cheap manipulation tactics. He wasn't playing a trick on her, trying to change her mind. He was being genuine, asking her a real question.

Georgia, of course, already knew the answer.

She turned the wheel and pulled the van over to the side of the road. She switched off the lights and the engine.

"So what's the plan?" she said.

"Let me think," said Max, peering towards the house.

The car was visible now. It was an early '90s Jeep. Georgia had actually considered purchasing one for herself, many years back. Instead, she'd gone with the pickups she'd always had. Georgia remembered that Max had had a similar car. She wasn't sure of the model, though, because by the time she'd seen it, it had been smashed, its metal twisted and its form unrecognizable.

"All right," said Max, speaking loudly. "I need everyone awake." He rapped his knuckles on the glass.

"What's going on?" came Chad's sleepy deep voice. The others groaned and yawned as they woke up.

"Are we in danger?" said Sadie, sounding worried.

"It's fine, Sadie," said Georgia. "We're just going to get some gas."

"Everyone awake?" said Max, turning around to see.

Max waited until each person answered.

"OK," said Max. "Here's the plan. We need gas. There's a car up there at the house. We're going to siphon it into our tank. James, I need you with me. You can move faster than I can with this leg. You OK with that, Georgia?"

"Yeah," said Georgia. She had her doubts and worries, but she knew that James was the best person for the job. He was young and quick. And he knew how to siphon gas. Georgia had showed him how once.

"Good. I'll keep guard. I need everyone else with their eyes peeled. I need someone looking in every direction, not just at the house. If anything goes wrong, we're getting out of here as fast as possible."

"We're just going to steal gas from someone?" said Mandy. "I don't think that's right."

"Those are the breaks," said Max. "We don't have any other options. If we don't get gas, we're stuck."

"But it's not right," said Mandy. "We might be preventing someone else from leaving, and saving their own life. Or their family's lives."

"That's right," said Max. "But we've got to do it. We're not going to take it by force. We'll be thieves in the night. Trust me, I'm not proud of it."

Mandy didn't say anything more.

"All right, Georgia," said Max. "Keep the lights off and creep up to that house. Get us right next to the Jeep. The gas cap is on the left side, facing the road."

"How do you know?"

"I had the same Jeep," said Max.

With the lights off, Georgia drove as slowly as she could. The van was almost silent. A Prius would have been ideal, but the van wasn't bad for keeping quiet. Not that Georgia would have ever been caught dead in a Prius in her past life. It just wasn't her scene. Now, though, everything had changed, and she'd drive anything if it meant keeping her family safe, from a Prius to a tractor.

They were going so slowly that it seemed to take forever. Finally, though, they were there. Georgia got as close as she could to the Jeep. She didn't need to worry about leaving enough space between the vehicles to open the doors. Max was already in the back. The sliding door would work no matter how little space there was.

"Perfect," said Max. "Keep the engine on in case we need to make a quick getaway. You ready, James?"

"Ready," said James.

Georgia knew her son well. She could hear the nervousness in his voice, even if the others couldn't. And she could tell he was trying to act brave and do the right thing. Georgia was proud of him, but she wished that his life could have become something else. A life where he didn't need to put on a brave face. He was just a teenager, after all.

"You have the hose?" said Max.

"Got it," said James.

Max had his gun in his hand as he slid open the minivan door. There was determination on his face, seen through the harsh shadows that the moon cast.

"Leave the door open," whispered Max. "Don't speak above a whisper, everyone."

The last thing Max did before getting out of the van was hand his multi-tool to James. "They might have put a lock on the gas cap door. But you can pry it open with this."

Georgia's job was to watch the house, to see if anyone came out. But it was hard. It was hard not to try to keep an eye on James, with the hose in his mouth.

Georgia heard James coughing and sputtering. He must have gotten the gas into his mouth. That was good. It'd be flowing by now, filling the plastic water sack.

"We shouldn't be doing this," whispered Mandy.

"Everyone watching?" whispered Georgia, ignoring Mandy's comment. "Everyone still awake?"

"Yeah," came all the replies.

"I'm worried, Mom," said Sadie, in a hushed voice.

"It's OK, Sadie," said Georgia. But they were empty words, and she knew it. Nothing was OK. But there was nothing else to say.

"Mom!" said Sadie, too loudly.

"Quiet," hissed Georgia.

"No, Mom, look! The house."

Georgia had been looking back at Sadie. She turned towards the house.

There was a light on in one of the downstairs rooms.

But that was impossible. The EMP had taken out everything. Not just the electrical grid, but the generators too.

At first, Georgia was too shocked to act.

The light shifted in the room, changing brightness. Then it hit her. It wasn't a normal light bulb. It was merely a high-powered flashlight. Someone was in there, moving around.

"James!" hissed Georgia, probably too loudly. "Max! There's someone coming."

No answer.

"Max!" hissed Georgia again.

"Just a little bit longer," came Max's reply.

"We've got to go. Now!"

"Just another moment… We've almost got it all."

Georgia was furious. Did Max really think a couple

gallons of extra gas were important in a moment like this? After all, her son's life was on the line. All their lives were on the line.

The door to the house swung open. A near-blinding beam of light swung over the van.

25

JOHN

Their eyes were locked.

John had had the luckiest break of his life, but it might not really do him any good.

John didn't know what to do. Should he try to escape? Up and out through the window? But he'd never make it in time. All this guy had to do was grab his legs.

But maybe he'd just stand there, jammed gun in hand, unmoving.

Of course, that wasn't going to happen.

He ran at John, moving suddenly. He moved his big, bulky body quickly.

As he ran, he swung the handgun like a hammer in a huge arc. It was coming right towards John's head.

There was only one thing for John to do. He moved to the side as best he could. He brought the knife up and stabbed with it, thrusting it forward with all his force.

The gun missed John's head. Instead, it smashed into his shoulder. Pain flared.

The knife went right into the man's chest. It went deep. It was sickening, how the knife penetrated the flesh so easily.

The man screamed.

John tugged the knife out, puling as hard as he could. It came free.

There was shouting upstairs. Heavy footsteps on the stairs again. More were coming down. It wouldn't take them long.

In a flash, hardly knowing what he was doing, John was at the window. He hoisted himself up, his hands cupping the concrete window sill. He had to let go with one hand in order to undo the latch and open the window. It opened outwards, leaving an impossibly narrow space. John didn't know if he could make it, but he was going to try.

He hoisted himself up further, his muscles straining.

Safety wasn't guaranteed on the other side of the window. Most probably, certain death awaited him, in the form of a man with a gun. But if he got outside, at least there was a chance. If he stayed in the basement, he'd die. That was *really* certain.

John squeezed himself through the window. He had to breathe in deeply to get through, and for a moment he thought he was stuck. But he pulled and pushed as hard as he possibly could, ignoring the horrible pain in his injured shoulder.

He heard noises behind him in the basement. He ignored them. It wasn't like he could turn around to see.

He finally broke free, squeezing himself out into the dark night.

A gunshot echoed in the basement. They'd fired at his feet, missing maybe by just an inch.

John looked around frantically, expecting a gun in his face.

But there was no one.

There wasn't time to think.

He simply ran, as fast and as hard as he could. He didn't know what direction he was headed in. He didn't know where he was going or what he would do next.

John felt his feet hit the pavement. He must have reached the street.

He kept running, knife in hand. He heard the door to the house swing open so forcefully that it slammed into the siding.

They were after him. And they had guns. They'd shoot him dead in the street like a dog.

Unless he could do something.

But what was there to do?

The sky was patchy with clouds, letting a substantial amount of moonlight through. If only the street had been darker, maybe they wouldn't be able to see him well enough to shoot him.

There was a dark patch off to the right. It was a small neighborhood park, full of tall trees with full leaves.

John's only hope was to get into that thick darkness, where the trees would shield him from the moonlight.

He didn't slow down as he turned, aiming towards the park.

A shot rang out. He didn't know if he'd made it yet to the darkness. There wasn't time to check, to analyze the light. He just kept running. He felt no pain except in his shoulder. They must have missed him.

John ran as fast and as hard as he could, for as long as he could. He ran through the park and he ran through empty suburban yards. He ran between houses and he ran across streets.

He didn't know if they were behind him. But he couldn't continue. He collapsed onto the ground, his breathing ragged and his heart thumping crazily with fear and exertion.

John lay on his back and looked up at the moon. He was too tired to check his surroundings, to see if he'd been followed, or if anyone else was there.

He knew he had to keep going. Not immediately. But soon.

The killings had been senseless. What had been gained by the deaths of Bill and the others? Maybe the militia had taken their guns, and the small amount of food and water they'd had with them. But surely that couldn't have been the real reason. From what Bill had said, the militia, or the various militias, were after one thing, and that was power. There were people who'd do anything to scramble to the top, no matter what the situation. No matter what was required, including killing.

And now, John was a wanted man. The suburbs had become enemy territory for him, and he was without supplies or backup. For just a moment, with Bill in the basement, there'd almost been a flicker of hope. A possibility that John could escape. But that had vanished. Bill was dead, and there was no hope that John was going to get out.

26

JOHN

Somehow, John had fallen asleep. He woke up with the early morning light. The birds were chirping as if the world hadn't ended, as if society hadn't collapsed.

John sat up, wincing in pain from his shoulder.

He was in a nice suburban backyard. There was a small in-ground pool, a glass outdoor table, lawn furniture. There was a croquet set, a couple hoses, and a small flower garden. Someone had planted something in a series of cinderblocks that lay against the back of the house.

By all appearances, it was a charming suburban backyard.

And it felt like a peaceful day. No lawnmower engines buzzed. No cars honked.

Then again, certainly no one was making coffee and reading the daily paper. No one was watching cartoons.

If there were people still in the house, they were hunkered down, probably in the basement or the attic, clutching whatever object they'd found that was the most weapon-like.

John cursed himself for falling asleep. He needed to keep moving. The smart thing to do would be to move by night. At least that way, he could try to avoid being seen by the militia. But in the broad daylight, what chance did he have? From what Bill had said, the militia controlled all the roads. And there wasn't any getting out of there without getting onto the roads at some point. There was only so far he could go through backyards.

John's kitchen knife lay next to him on the grass. The blade was coated in dried blood, and John carefully wiped it along the dewy grass, cleaning the blade. The kitchen knife had become his only reliable companion. When he'd left his apartment, he'd never thought he'd last long at all. And a lot of that "lasting" had to do with his knife. Well, that and dumb luck.

John shouldn't have been alive. He'd made four "friends" so far since his apartment, if you could really call them that. And he'd seen each one killed before his eyes. Why did John deserve to live and they didn't?

But he pushed those thoughts away. There was no sense in dwelling on that now. In doing so, John had another thought: his own thinking process was changing. That was natural. The EMP aftermath had shaped and molded his brain. Intense experiences tended to do that. John was noticing that slowly, little by little, he was becoming more practical minded. This way of thinking reminded him of his brother Max, who always looked to the practical first. Or at least what Max considered the practical.

John needed a place to hide out for the day. He wasn't going to risk traveling far during the daylight. Not after what he'd seen yesterday.

He didn't dare try to enter this house here. There was no way to know whether it was abandoned or not.

If he tried to enter, there was a good chance he'd be attacked by the occupants. John didn't want to fight some innocent family trying desperately to hold on. He was now willing to fight, but not like that. He'd fight people who came after him, who tried to take his own life away.

The thought of entering the house, though, was tempting. Inside, there might be food, water, a place to rest comfortably.

But it wouldn't work. He couldn't risk it.

John moved over to the cinderblocks. The plants growing inside looked odd. Long green stems. But no flowers. They triggered a distant memory. He'd seen them somewhere before.

On a hunch, John dug down into the earth. His instinct had been right. Down in the dirt, potatoes were growing. He'd heard about this before—some trend of growing food inside cinderblocks. He didn't get it, but he didn't need to.

John dug until he'd recovered all the potatoes. There was another batch of cinderblocks, and John dug through those. These didn't contain potatoes. Instead, under the leaves, John found small wilted-looking peppers. He picked these as well.

He couldn't eat just yet. Instead, he surveyed the area, hoping to find somewhere to hide out.

In the yard next door, there was a small shed. Maybe that would work. He could hide out in there until nightfall. He'd need some luck, though. There was a good chance someone might enter the shed, looking for something useful, like gasoline or other supplies.

John had to climb over a fence to get to the next yard. He threw his handful of potatoes and peppers over the fence first, and then hoisted himself over. His shoulder still burned with pain from getting smacked by the gun.

He wished he had that gun. But there hadn't been time to think of things like that. If he'd gone for the gun, there was a good chance he'd have been shot trying to get it, or trying to get out the window.

John gathered up his potatoes and peppers. He was so hungry that his mouth was salivating as he scooped them up. The smell of the peppers was intense and delicious, and John didn't even like peppers. It was hard for him not to sit down right there and eat everything. That was how hungry he was.

Fortunately, the shed was unlocked.

It was dark inside, and cramped. He couldn't see much at all at first. Only a little bit of light came in through a couple gaps where the roof hadn't been fitted correctly to the walls. It wasn't one of those quality Amish sheds that many in Pennsylvania had. It was just some cheapo knock off, assembled hastily and poorly. But that worked in John's favor now, since gradually, his eyes adjusted the darkness and soon enough he could see fairly well.

John didn't waste any time. He ate the potatoes first. They were raw, of course, but he bit into them like apples, eating the skin and everything. His stomach started to ache almost right away, but he ignored it. It was more important to get food into his stomach than worry about whether or not the raw potatoes might make him sick.

Next, he ate the peppers. Normally, he hated spicy food. But the potatoes hadn't been nearly enough. After all, when was the last time he'd eaten? There'd been that stale bread, but that didn't have any protein. And then there'd been that bar food. Not much protein there either.

John remembered reading that potatoes actually contained high quality protein. They didn't show up on the normal nutrition charts as high-protein foods, however, because the protein content was normally measured against the whole weight of the potatoes, including the water. The article John had read had mentioned that during lean times in Ireland, workers were known to survive on nothing but potatoes. Of course, John didn't know whether he'd be able to effectively assimilate the protein in raw potatoes. Judging by his stomach cramps, there were some problematic components of the potatoes that were normally neutralized by cooking.

Whatever, he couldn't worry about that now.

The peppers stung his mouth horribly. They were incredibly hot. John didn't know what type of peppers they were, except that they were an orange-red and incredibly shriveled looking. He was pretty sure that the more shriveled a pepper appeared, the hotter it was on whatever index it was that the experts used to measure spiciness.

For a long while, perhaps hours, John sat with his back against the cheap plywood shed wall. His mouth burned, since there was nothing to wash the peppers down with. His back ached, his shoulder and stomach hurt, and his legs were cramping up, since there was no room to stretch them out.

But at least he was safe for now.

Relatively safe.

Finally, John's legs couldn't take it anymore. He had to stretch them.

He was nervous about making any noise that could be heard outside the shed, in case someone was nearby. He had no way to know if someone was inches away from him on the other side of the shed walls. He doubted he'd be able to hear soft footsteps on the grass.

So far, though, he hadn't heard any noises at all. Nothing but the birds.

John set about rearranging the things in the shed as quietly as he could. It seemed as if no one had been inside it in years. There was a thick layer of dusty grime over most things, and soon John's fingers and hands were filthy.

There was an old lawnmower in one corner, along with a plastic gas can that made the whole shed smell like gas and made John even more nauseated than he already felt. The half-opened cans of paint and lacquer didn't help either.

John suddenly realized that having gas inside the shed could be bad. Really bad. Surely people would need gas now, more than ever before. Someone was bound to start entering sheds, looking for gas.

But maybe he'd be lucky. Maybe no one would come.

As John was rearranging things, moving them as slowly and quietly as he could, stacking them on top of one another, he realized he should be looking for things that could be useful to him. He felt dumb for not thinking of it earlier.

There wasn't bound to be food in the shed, but there had to be something he could use... some sort of weapon, maybe, or some flashlights. If he could find some old camping gear, maybe that would help him.

It took John at least another hour to find what he was looking for. He'd finally arranged all the old rotten wood in one corner. He'd gotten all the rusty gardening tools together and put them above the wood. He'd taken a long hoe that seemed like it was well made and set it aside, thinking he might take it with him. The handle was a strong, dense wood, and the metal head, while a little rusty, seemed like it was well made, of real steel. It was one of those old tools, from back when things were made properly. The edge had been maintained and sharpened over the years, possibly obsessively, until it had been left to sit unused in the shed for who knew how long. It'd probably been used for edging work. John cut his finger as he ran it across the blade.

John could use it as a weapon and a walking stick.

There was also a hatchet, completely covered in rust. It was one of those classic hatchets, the kind they'd sold in hardware stores across the country for decades. They cost about $25 and worked fine, but they weren't very stain resistant. Taking an edge wasn't their strong suit, but it would do the job, even with the rust and imperfect edge.

The hatchet could be a good weapon. And if John ever got into the woods, out of the suburbs, maybe he could use it to build a shelter. That was the sort of thing Max would have thought of. And this was the time when thinking like Max, well, it was just the right way to think about things.

John didn't find the payload for another twenty minutes, moving everything around so slowly and delicately, conscious of the noise, always listening for approaching footsteps or the sound of an engine.

Underneath a dirt-caked tarp, there it was.

An ancient backpack. Looked like army surplus, maybe. It was the kind of pack that hippy kids used to use to hitchhike around the US in the '70s.

The pack seemed full. John tried not to get his hopes up. For all he knew, maybe it was just filled with trash, empty liquor bottles or something, a memento of a misspent youth long ago.

He almost couldn't believe it when he opened up the pack.

Inside, it appeared to be completely full of camping gear.

There was an ancient tent, large and bulky. But it fit inside the pack just fine.

There were two water bottles, full of stale water. Who knew how old the water was.

There was a small emergency medical kit, and a bottle of prescription sleeping pills. Best of all, the rest of the pack was filled with energy bars. They had old labels on them, with graphics that made John think they'd been produced sometime in the mid to late '90s.

The contents of the pack were strange. John's best guess was that about twenty years ago, someone had packed up their old backpack for a camping trip that they never ended up taking. After that, the bag had stayed, still packed, forgotten in the shed.

There wasn't much else in the pack. It wasn't complete by any sense of the imagination. But it would be enough.

John immediately went for the water. He smelled it first, and it had a strange odor to it. But he figured it was a risk he'd have to take. He took his first sip and almost spit it out.

But John realized that the majority of the strange taste was most likely coming from the aluminum of the water bottle seeping into the water. He could deal with a little aluminum. It wasn't like he'd die from that any time soon, if at all. And if there was bacteria in the water? Well, he'd deal with that too. It was better than dying of thirst.

He had to force himself not to drink the whole bottle at once. Who knew when the next time he'd get water was.

John tore into one of the energy bars, which had gone hard and stale over the years. But it didn't smell too strange, and it actually still tasted good. It had a lot of sugar in it, and John wouldn't have been able to describe how intensely pleasing the taste of real sugar was in that moment. It seemed to warm his body and give him more mental strength to continue.

Now he had gear. Maybe he actually stood a chance.

Now all he had to do was get out of the suburbs and not get discovered. That was going to be hard, if not impossible.

But he'd try.

John dozed off once or twice during the rest of the day, but mostly he just waited. He tried his best to think of a plan, to map out a route. But his thinking wasn't as clear as he would have liked. Probably from the intense stress he was feeling. He just couldn't seem to conjure up a picture of a map in his head.

The best thing to do was simply try. He'd head through the yard and parks as much as he could, keeping off of the roads. He'd eventually make his way far enough north that the suburbs would give way to the more rural areas. Then, he'd stay away from the highways and roads and stay well within the woods, hidden from prying eyes by the trees and thick late summer foliage.

If he made it that far, his biggest problem might simply be finding the farmhouse. He didn't have a map, and he hadn't been to the farmhouse since he was a kid. He vaguely remembered what the area looked like. But it wasn't like he'd ever actually driven up there himself. He'd been a kid, riding in the back seat with Max. His parents, obviously, had done all the navigating.

It seemed like a long shot. Almost impossible. Then again, maybe he'd see something along the way that would give him a clue to where he was and where he needed to go. Maybe he'd come across some landmark.

That was all based on the hope that he wouldn't simply die in the woods.

The day seemed to stretch forever, with nothing to do

but stare at the walls, make seemingly futile plans, and re-check his newfound gear over and over.

Finally, it was nightfall. There were still no sounds outside the shed.

John waited through dusk, growing increasingly impatient. Why couldn't the sun just set faster? Did it really have to take its sweet time going down? Didn't it need a rest like everyone else?

Maybe John's thoughts were turning a little strange. Then again, maybe it was normal. Since the EMP, John had probably spent more time alone than he had in a long, long time. His work life involved dealing with people constantly, and he wasn't the type to stay at home by himself. He'd always been out and about, with a hot date on his arm and money in his pocket.

John had read stories about people in extreme situations, people who'd had to fight for their lives. He remembered a story about a man who'd been stuck at sea for six months, living off seagull meat and blood. When he'd eventually been rescued, he'd been unrecognizable to his family. Not that his appearance had changed much. Instead, it was his personality. He was just different. A human can't go through such a harrowing experience and come out the other side the same person. It's just not possible.

But that man at sea had a civilization to come back to.

John didn't.

And no one else did either.

Maybe whatever changes John was going through mentally, they'd be permanent ones. And maybe that wasn't so bad. He was adapting to his new environment. He'd killed it in the financial field, and now those skills didn't serve him anymore. Maybe it was a testament to his character that he was able to make the changes necessary, even if he was doing a clumsy amateur job of the whole thing so far.

In the silent darkness, John got his things together. He hoisted the ancient backpack onto his shoulders. It was heavy, and his shoulder hurt from the strap.

He tucked the rusted hatchet into one of the straps on the side of the backpack. He put his kitchen knife in an odd sort of pocket that someone must have sewn onto the side of the backpack. It fit in there nicely, and with a little luck, he'd be able to reach it easily.

One hand was free, and the other held the long hoe.

His heart was pounding in his chest as he finally reached for the handle to the door of the shed.

It was time to continue his journey.

27

MAX

"Get away from my car," shouted the man in the door of the house.

"Keep going," whispered Max to James.

James obeyed him, holding the plastic tubing through which the gasoline flowed.

"We've got to go!" hissed Georgia from inside the minivan.

But Max knew they needed to wait. They needed that gas more than anything. It was worth the risk. It was worth the danger.

Max wasn't going to risk James's young life, though.

Glock in hand, Max stood up from behind the Jeep, making himself visible. He wanted to make himself the target, and not James.

Maybe it was dumb. Maybe it was the dumbest thing he'd ever done. And at the start of the EMP, Max had been the guy who'd just been interested in looking out for himself. His attitude couldn't have changed quicker.

"Get off my property," shouted the man in the doorway.

His flashlight blinded Max. He tried to shield his eyes, but the flashlight was too bright.

"It's dumb to waste your batteries on us," said Max loudly. "You're using the brightest setting. Turbo mode, probably. Won't last more than ten minutes. I know my flashlights."

Max was just stalling for time. He wasn't actually concerned about whether the man burned up his flashlight batteries or not.

"I've got a gun," shouted the man.

Max could hear the fear in his voice. He had a strong hunch that he wouldn't shoot.

Then again, everything was different know. People were doing things they'd never have done before.

And fear could propel people to do things they'd normally never dream of.

"Got it all," whispered James.

Max heard James pulling the tube from the Jeep.

"Make sure you get the tube," whispered Max out of the side of his mouth.

"We're leaving," said Max loudly. "There's no need for any violence."

Max backed up slowly. He made sure James had gotten into the minivan before he himself did.

Max's heart was thumping in his chest as he slowly got into the van. It felt like an impossibly long moment, a moment in which Max could easily take a bullet from the stranger.

But he didn't shoot. Max's instincts had been right.

"Go," said Max.

The van was already moving. Georgia was on the ball.

She was driving fast, headlights back on, down the

narrow country road. There was nothing in front of them, and just dark trees on either side.

"You could have both gotten killed," said Georgia.

She sounded angry. Max knew she had every reason to be. Max had put her son, not to mention all of them, in danger. But he'd weighed the risks against the final outcome. It had paid off, but it easily could have gone the other way.

Max would take the blame. And he was OK with that.

"We needed the gas," said Max.

"James could have been shot," said Georgia. "And you could have prevented it. It was his neck on the line."

She sounded angrier than Max had ever heard her. It wasn't like her. She had a good understand of necessity, and James had been in danger before. But Max could understand why this particular situation would bother her more than others. To her, it had probably seemed as if Max was being intentionally reckless.

"Mom," said James, piping up. "It's OK. Nothing happened. And Max actually put himself on the line... He stood up. He would have been the one to get shot. Not me."

Georgia didn't say anything more. But no one else spoke, and the atmosphere in the van was tense for the next hour or so until the sun started to come up.

Max was busy doing mental calculations around their gas usage. The minivan wasn't running as efficiently as it should have, and they'd need more gas soon. Maybe they could make it another eight hours of solid driving, and maybe they couldn't.

And there was no guarantee that when they eventually got low again on gas that there'd be another situation that allowed them to refuel.

No one in the car was asleep, and various foods from the

Millers were passed around. They all agreed to save the beef jerky as much as possible, since they'd need protein along the way. But it was hard to do, since they all found it the most appetizing thing to eat. Maybe their bodies were giving them signals through their cravings, telling them that they needed more protein.

The best thing to do would be to keep their eyes peeled for another car to siphon gas from. They could fill up the water sack and carry the gas with them in the van. That way, they'd have more of a choice in when they decided to put their necks on the line again, rather than waiting for the gas to run out.

Max knew it wouldn't be a popular idea. He knew Georgia wouldn't like it. But it made the most sense, and he was going to speak his mind no matter how it was taken.

"Listen," said Max, breaking the silence that seemed to echo through the minivan. "We're going to need more gas soon enough... and..." He explained his thinking.

Of course, Georgia objected.

"I don't see why it's any less risky to get the gas sooner rather than later," said Georgia.

"It lets us choose the situation," said Max. "It gives us more of a strategic advantage."

"It didn't do us much good before."

She was still mad. But that was OK with Max. He understood.

"I think Max is right," said James.

"He's got a good point," said Mandy. "It's going to be dangerous either way. We might as well have some advantage."

"I don't see what difference it makes," said Chad. "I don't see any other cars anyway. We haven't driven past a house in miles."

"We passed one a ways back," said Mandy. "You were just asleep."

Just then, a car appeared in front of them, coming around a blind curve. Its headlights were on, despite the rising sun.

"Shit," muttered Georgia. "Let's hope this goes well."

"Just keep driving," said Max.

Georgia had to slow down because of the curve. They couldn't have been going more than twenty-five miles an hour. The other car wasn't going quickly either. It was an older SUV, and as it got closer Max recognized it as a Ford Bronco.

"What do you think I should do?" said Georgia.

"Hopefully they'll just drive right on by," said Mandy. "That's what the others did."

The two vehicles passed one another, going slowly.

Max turned to look.

Inside, there were two men wearing light jackets. Their heads were almost shaved. One of them had a tattoo running up his neck. It reminded Max of the convicts who'd attacked him in the woods heading to the farmhouse.

The men stared right into the minivan. There was cruelty in their faces.

"Are they going to kill us?" said Sadie weakly.

No one answered.

The moment had only lasted for an instant. The minivan was past them now.

"Let's just hope they don't turn around," said Max. He turned around himself, to get a better look. Everyone else turned too, craning their heads.

Just before the minivan was about to disappear around the bend in the road, the Ford Bronco's brake lights went on, a bright red in the early morning light.

The last thing Max saw before they rounded the corner was the Bronco slowing down to a complete stop.

"Shit," muttered Max. "I think they're turning around."

"What can we do about it?" said Chad.

"Not much," said Max. "There don't seem to be a lot of turn offs on this road. And I doubt we can park somewhere and hide..."

"Drive faster, Mom," said Sadie.

"It's not going to do any good," said Max. "We'll have to face them sooner or later. But we have the advantage. We outnumber them. Now where are those semi-automatics?"

Max was moving around as best he could with his injured leg, squeezing between people's legs. He was looking for the two semi automatic guns that they'd taken from the men who'd attacked the farmhouse.

"Where are they?" said Max. "Help me look, everyone."

Georgia was driving fast.

So far, the Ford Bronco hadn't appeared around the bend.

On one hand, two guys against everyone in the minivan wouldn't be much of a fight. On the other hand, they might have some tricks up their sleeves that Max and the others weren't expecting. And Max knew well that they themselves weren't experienced fighters. They'd seen the devastation only a few men could cause back at the farmhouse.

Max and Georgia were good shots. James was getting there. But the rest? Who knew. They had the instincts to protect themselves, but they didn't yet have the ability to use a firearm consistently under pressure. One shot might hit its target, and the next might be a mile off. And there was no telling what order that might happen in.

Everyone but Georgia was scrambling around, looking for the guns.

"How could we have lost them?" said Max. "This doesn't make sense."

The semi-automatics would give them a huge advantage. Hunting rifles weren't ideal for a serious confrontation.

"We had them at the Millers'," said Max. "Right?"

"Yeah," said Chad. "We brought them with us. I remember, because it was hard as shit carrying all those guns. But you didn't want us to leave any of them in the van."

"Uh," said Sadie, her voice quiet. "I think we might have left them at the Millers'. I remember seeing one on the way out... I thought it was their own gun at the time."

No one said anything.

The bend in the road was well in the distance now. But Max could still see well enough to spot the Ford Bronco when it came slowly around the corner. Max felt his blood turning cold as the adrenaline shot through him. They were going to have to fight, and only with their rifles and Max's handgun. Who knew what the men in the Bronco had at their disposal.

"Shit," muttered Max. "They're after us."

"Maybe they just realized they took a wrong turn or something," said Chad. "It's probably hella hard finding your way around these parts."

"Shut up, Chad," said Mandy. "Unless you have something useful to say."

"What?" said Chad. "I'm just trying to be positive."

"They're after us," said Mandy. "Why else would they turn around?"

Max didn't say anything. Instead, he found the binoculars from the men who'd attacked the farmhouse. He strung them around his neck as he moved to the very back of the van.

With the binoculars, Max could see their faces. They

had that same vicious look he'd seen when they'd passed. Other than that, he couldn't see anything else that gave them any more information than what they already had. There were no guns visible. No other weapons either.

The Ford Bronco continued to follow them at a great distance. Without the binoculars, they looked far, far away, almost too far to see, unless you knew what to look for.

Everyone was talking all at once. Arguing, trying to speak above one another. The appearance of the Bronco had sent pulses racing and emotions changing. Chad and Mandy were in the middle of a heated argument. James and Sadie had their own argument, but they occasionally interjected between Chad and Mandy.

Max didn't pay it any attention. Neither did Georgia. They were the only two who didn't speak.

"What's the plan, Max?" said Georgia finally, from the driver's seat.

"Drive," said Max. "That's all we can do for now. Everyone else, get your rifles ready."

28

JOHN

John had been walking through the suburbs for what felt like hours. But he had no way of knowing the time.

The sky was cloudy, blocking the moonlight. The suburbs were dark. There were no streetlights. No ambient light from homes. No light coming from Philadelphia.

So far, John hadn't run into anyone. He hadn't seen a soul.

Once, he'd heard the rumbling of a truck, probably a diesel. John hadn't waited to find out who it was or what they wanted. It was probably the rogue militia. John had ducked into a nearby backyard, hopped a fence, and moved a whole street over, changing his direction from north to east.

After a while, he'd gotten out of earshot of the truck, and he started heading north again.

It was hard to keep track of which way he was headed. He remembered how to find the North Star. He'd been taught it as a boy, and for some reason the information had always stuck with him. It had seemed like a neat trick at the time. Now, his life could depend on it. Unfortunately, there was no North Star visible tonight with the heavy clouds.

So he relied instead on his knowledge of the layout of the streets. He knew the pattern well.

At least, he hoped he knew it well.

He was hoping he was heading north again. But he wouldn't know until he reached Route 30.

He knew he was south of Route 30. Once he crossed over it, he'd know he'd been heading in the right direction. Route 30 ran east from Philadelphia to Lancaster and beyond. It ran right through the Main Line, running parallel to the train line for which the area was named.

Once or twice, John saw candle lights flickering in houses. Mostly, though, there was nothing but tightly drawn curtains. Many of the driveways had cars still in them. Many people must have stayed home, not trying to flee. Or maybe they had, and they'd encountered some roadblock and returned to the relative safety of their home. There, though, they were likely to starve to death. Or meet some even worse fate.

The horrors of the new world in which John found himself had started to lose some of their intensity. John no longer found himself surprised when he saw something horrible, or when he thought of the horrors that the people here would soon face. Everything had somehow been softened for him. It was because of what he'd been through. He knew that and he was aware of it. His mind was recalibrating itself, as human minds do. He was adapting.

But he didn't know if that was good or not.

John only found one dead body. John didn't feel anything when he looked at the body. The horrors so far had sapped his compassion completely.

He peered down to examine her, merely out of strategic curiosity. It was a woman in her early 40s. Everything that she'd possibly had of value had been stripped from her. She lay there in mud-stained shorts and ripped t-shirt. Her shoes were missing, and there were marks on her neck. It looked as if someone had forcefully torn a necklace off her. On her fingers, there were marks from where a ring, probably a wedding ring, had rested for a long time.

The thing that should have disturbed John the most was that her skull had been broken open. But he merely studied it, trying to determine the cause of the injury.

He was disturbed by his lack of emotional response. He also knew that he had almost met a similar fate many times. Possibly a similar fate awaited him in the future.

There was no way to know. He was gradually developing his own strange sort of Zen philosophy about the whole situation. Maybe it was his own attempt to deal with what had happened, and to deal with his decreasing sensitivity. Maybe it was just his mind, unused to solitude, running in a different way than it ever had before.

In the city, he'd lost track of how many bodies he'd stepped over and walked past.

But there were more people there. And things had happened faster than out here.

Soon enough, there would be more bodies. And there was nothing John could do about that. He couldn't change the fates of those here. He couldn't help them.

The only thing he could do was to try to look out for himself.

John had come up from fairly far south, from where the Schuylkill River had taken him. He breathed a sigh of relief when he saw the unmistakable Route 30 ahead of him.

He had emerged from cutting through an apartment

complex into an area that was less residential and more commercial. There was a gym, a gas station, and a small mini mart.

John approached Route 30 cautiously. It was a large four lane road. Normally, it was jammed with traffic at all hours of the day. Now, there wasn't a car to be seen.

At least not from where he stood.

But when he moved forward, crossing the road, he saw something about a mile down. He stopped in the middle of the empty road and peered down. He couldn't quite make out what it was. But it looked a lot like a military blockade. There was a large truck blocking at least part of the road, parked perpendicular to the lanes.

John hurried across the road, taking cover in some bushes on the other side. He hoped that no one had seen him. He waited, unmoving, crouched in the bushes, for ten minutes before he decided to move on.

Heading north, there was a long curvy road that ran up a large hill, towards Valley Forge Park. Beyond that, there was the King of Prussia Mall, which at one point had been the largest in the country. Maybe it was the third largest now. John couldn't remember, not that it mattered much anymore.

John followed the road, staying parallel to it. He moved through backyards, keeping as far away from the houses as he could. If he made sure to follow the road, there wasn't a chance that he wouldn't be heading north. That was an advantage given the cloudy sky.

John didn't stop to eat or drink anything, even though he was hungry and thirsty. He knew it was important to get as far away from the suburbs as possible while he still could.

Up ahead, there were two possible routes. John could cut through Valley Forge Park, where George Washington had camped out for a winter with his men, avoiding the British who had occupied Philadelphia. Or he could cut through the mall and surrounding area. There were houses around Valley Forge, but there were also huge swathes of open land that he could hide out in. It could be a good place, but then again… who knew what could be waiting for him there in the woods.

John remembered going to Valley Forge as a kid with Max. They'd somehow gotten hold of some fireworks that were illegal in Pennsylvania. Maybe a friend had bought them on a family trip or something. John couldn't remember now, and it didn't matter anyway. But he thought about it as he walked, and tried to remember. The memory wouldn't come. Another one of those lost moments. Seemed appropriate for a lost civilization.

Or almost lost. John wondered if there'd ever be a chance to rebuild. So far, things had gotten so far out of hand so quickly that he didn't see how it would be possible. At least not for a long, long while.

Valley Forge was only about fifteen miles from Philadelphia, far enough away that it had given Washington and his troops a safe haven. The way the landscape had worked, they would have seen the British coming from miles away. But that was long ago. What had been farmland then had been developed.

John's other option was to cut through the King of Prussia Mall area. Its advantage was that there weren't many homes there. That could cut the risk of exposure—the fewer people there were the less likely John was to be seen.

There were a lot of stores in the King of Prussia area. That meant a lot of goods. John knew there were hiking and camping stores. There were probably plenty of people who'd had the idea to head to those stores in search of things to help them survive. Maybe the rogue militia was there. Maybe there were other dangers John hadn't even considered.

He had a little while to decide. The road was long. His shoulder was killing him. His back ached too, from the weight of the pack. The hoe helped as a walking stick. He was able to transfer some of the weight of the pack onto it with every other step.

There was a rumbling on the road. The sound of engines. Someone was approaching.

John crouched down behind a large rose bush. He was in the backyard of a stone home. It wasn't unusual for homes in the area to be 200 years old or more, and this one could easily have been that old. It was nicely maintained, with a tidy garden. There weren't drawn curtains on this home, and there was no vehicle in the driveway. Likely, the occupants had left.

John briefly considered whether he should break into the home to hide out for the coming day. He didn't know the time, but if he had to guess, he would have said it was about three in the morning. There were still a couple good hours of hiking through the night. It was better to get farther away than to stay here. But it wasn't like the rose bush was the greatest hiding place.

John waited too long making up his mind. Before he knew it, the sounds were closer than ever.

They must have been trucks. Large, heavy trucks. He felt the rumbling beneath his feet.

To John's horror, the trucks stopped somewhere nearby. He couldn't see them. The house was blocking the way. He could hear them, rumbling, the engines clearly idling. The engines cut off, leaving silence.

Then came the shouts. Orders being barked out. Brusque and crude.

Gunshots, loud, in quick succession.

Horrible screaming. Calls for help.

The truck engines started again. John heard the trucks driving off.

It had all happened so fast. John barely had time to process it all.

He knew he should stay behind the bush. But the cries for help continued. The soldiers, or whoever they were, seemed to have left in the trucks, leaving behind their victims.

John stood up. He had a choice. Did he move on, cutting through the next yard, or did he go address the screams?

He thought of Lawrence, who had died in his arms. John didn't know whether Lawrence's insistence on helping people had been foolish or not. He'd thought it was, and he'd convinced Lawrence to leave the city. That was what had gotten him killed. Then again, he surely would have died had he stayed...

John walked to the road, working his way through the tidy gardens that lined the side yard of the old stone house.

Across the road, there was a woman in the front yard. She bent over a man who lay on the ground.

"Help me!" she yelled, spotting John.

Why did she think John was someone she could trust? For all she knew, he could be someone who wanted to further harm her and her family.

John didn't know why, but he rushed across the street, setting his backpack down to bend over the man.

The woman had tears streaming down her face. Her hair was tangled. Blood was on her hands from holding the man. He must have been her husband. And he was dead. There wasn't any way to save him. His eyes were open and he wasn't breathing. He lay still on his back, blood all over his torso. The spurts of gunfire had torn open his chest and stomach.

"I'm sorry," said John. "He's dead." It felt strange stating the obvious.

"He can't be dead, he just can't."

There was nothing more to say. John didn't need to convince her that he was dead.

John put his arm around her shoulder. He didn't tell her that everything was going to be OK. He couldn't bring himself to utter those words.

"I can't believe it. I just can't believe it."

"He was your husband?"

She nodded. Her face was red and blotchy from the tears. Her body was shaking. John tightened his arm around her, pulling her close to him.

Maybe he should have moved her away from the corpse. That was what people did sometimes after tragedies, soothing their emotions by removing them from the body. She was staring into her dead husband's lifeless eyes. The body was a reminder of the horrors that had just passed, and the horrors that would pass. John didn't see the point in shielding her from reality. Sooner or later, they'd all have to face it.

"What happened?" said John.

"They came," she said, between sobs. "Yesterday. They came yesterday. They wanted food and... John wouldn't give them what they wanted... They said they were being nice... They'd give us one more day... I pleaded with him, but he said we'd die without it..."

So her husband was named John as well. What a strange coincidence.

"You don't have any food?"

"None," she said, shaking her head. The tears still hadn't stopped and her body still shook violently. "They took everything… Everything…"

Comforting her wouldn't do any good. She could come to terms with her husband's death and she'd still be dead soon enough without food.

"Do you have any family around here? Children? Any friends?"

She shook her head.

It was all too common not to know one's neighbors. John remembered his own situation back at his apartment in Center City, the apartment he'd never see again.

John had become somewhat desensitized to death and violence. That didn't mean that he had no reaction whatsoever to the dead body on the ground in front of him. It just didn't hit him hard like it should have. Truthfully, it barely hit him at all.

But while his emotions had become blunted, something else had changed in him. John had always looked out for himself. He'd looked after his own money, his apartments, his clothes. He'd had his own best interests in mind, and no one else's. He'd mocked Lawrence's attitude, and had brought Lawrence along only to serve his own ends.

It wasn't like now he was going to try to go and save the whole world. It was impossible. But maybe while trying to save himself, he could help one single person. This woman, who'd lost her husband. Why didn't she deserve a chance?

"Come with me," said John.

"What?"

"I'm getting out of here," said John. "I'm heading north. My brother has a farmhouse. I'm sure he's there, with the whole place set up with everything he needs. I don't know if

I'm going to make it up there. But at least there's a chance. Come with me. Maybe we'll make it out of here."

She just looked at him. Her sobbing slowed down.

"You're going to die here," said John. "Without food, you won't make it. And the militia will keep killing, even when it doesn't make any sense. I don't think many will survive here."

John didn't know what to expect, whether she'd say yes or no.

Finally, after a long pause, she nodded her head silently at him.

John stood up and offered the woman his hand.

Taking her along would have its risks. But John would be lying if he told himself he was only doing it as some type of selfless sacrifice. Sure, he wanted to help her. But that self-serving part of himself still did exist somewhere inside him, albeit in smaller quantities than before. Two people instead of one definitely had its advantages. It meant one person could keep watch while the other slept. It meant two people to fight, not just one.

29

GEORGIA

They'd been driving a full two hours in tense silence. The Bronco kept following. No matter how fast or slow Georgia drove, the Bronco was there behind them. It kept its distance. Sometimes Georgia could see it in the mirror and sometimes she couldn't. But when she couldn't, and she hoped for a brief moment that the nightmare was over, Max in the back with his binoculars would confirm that it was still there.

Georgia couldn't believe that the semi-automatics had been left at the Millers'. It was a huge oversight, even given their emergency exit. No one had been blamed. No one knew whose fault it was, or if it was anyone's at all. After all, it wasn't like the guns had been assigned to anyone in particular. No one had a designated responsibility.

They'd made so many mistakes in the last weeks. Leaving the guns behind was just another grave error in a long list of them. They'd set up a horrible watch system at the farmhouse, one that had almost cost them their lives. They should have had more people on watch, at all times.

There were too many "should haves" to even mentally list. And they couldn't be correct now. Only in the future.

Georgia was trying to keep herself as calm as possible. She knew that ruminating on what they'd done wrong would only increase her pulse, only make her sweat. And above all, make her less effective when the time to act eventually came.

She was worried about James and Sadie. She was worried about them all. But James and Sadie the most.

The gas gauge had dipped almost to half. They seemed to be burning fuel faster than earlier. Maybe something was wrong with the van. Not that they could stop to check on the engine. Not now.

Georgia had taken the first turn she could. The Bronco had followed. She'd taken another turn, and again the Bronco had followed.

Now they were lost.

"What are we going to do?" said Mandy, sounding frantic.

"We're screwed," said Sadie.

"Don't use that language," said Georgia. She said it automatically. Honestly, she didn't care what kind of language Sadie used now. And Sadie was probably right, anyway.

"We'll be fine," said Chad. "We can take them. Let's just stop. I mean, come on, they're going to come up against six of us? We've all got guns and we know how to use 'em."

"Some of us know how to use them better than others," said Mandy.

"You think I don't know how to shoot?" said Chad. "What about that guy I shot from the roof?"

"Took you long enough, didn't it?" said Mandy.

"What are we going to do, Max?" said Georgia.

Everyone got quiet. They expected Max to be the voice of reason. They expected him to be the one with the plan.

"We're going to have to face them at some point," said Max. "We've got... a couple hours at least until we're out of state. Maybe more now that we're lost."

"I don't have any clue where we are," said Georgia. "Any ideas, Mandy?" Mandy was the one who'd spent the most time with the maps. Georgia had never come to this part of the state on her hunting trips.

"No idea," said Mandy.

Great, that was just great.

"We're bound to come to a town sooner or later," said Georgia. "And that's going to bring its own host of problems."

"Maybe the problems will cancel each other out?" said James. "You know, like in math class? We run into some bad guys in a town, and then the Bronco guys decide they don't want to mess with us."

"This isn't math class, James," said Sadie.

"Shut up, I know that."

"It might work," said Max. "But I doubt it. We can't risk it. We're going to have to pull over and face them sooner or later."

"What do you think our chances are?" said Georgia.

"Not good," said Max.

"Chad has a point, though," said Georgia. "We outnumber them."

"Right," said Max. "But they know that. They saw how many people we have when they passed us. And they wouldn't be following us unless they thought they were sure they could take us all out."

"What does that mean? Semi-automatics?"

"Not sure," said Max. "Either that, or something else

we're not thinking of. Maybe they're ex-military. Or maybe they have some other kind of training. Or maybe they're just irrational or crazy, which could be equally as dangerous."

Georgia knew that Max was making good points, and it sent a chill down her spine.

"The thing we're forgetting," said Max. "Or not taking into account—however you want to put it—is that when we talk about outnumbering them, we're still talking about some of us dying. Or at least getting shot. That's the most likely outcome. We've got to face the fact that while there are a lot of us, we're not skilled fighters. These guys might be. At this point, we all know basic gun safety, and things like that. But most of us don't have extensive experience with firearms."

Max knew that he wasn't speaking for himself, or for Georgia. He was being diplomatic about their abilities, even in a crisis situation. She didn't know what to think about that. Maybe he was just trying to stop infighting amongst them during this crisis, because it wasn't like Max not to say things directly. He liked to say it how it was, when possible.

"What are we going to do then?" said Mandy. "We're just going to let them follow us until we need gas and then let them attack us?"

"We don't yet know what they want," said Max.

"What does that matter? We know they're following us. They want to hurt us."

"Probably," said Max. "But it's possible that they want something of ours."

"So what? I don't see what difference that makes," said Mandy.

"Well," said Max. "There's always the lost art of diplomacy."

"Diplomacy? Are you crazy? You want to negotiate with them?"

"I admit it's not ideal," said Max. "But as far as last options go, it's not the worst thing that comes to mind."

Georgia didn't know what to think of Max's plan.

"Are you serious, Max?" said Georgia.

"Yeah," said Max. "Now I'm not asking anyone else to do it. I'll volunteer. I say we stop, and I'll see if I can get them to stay at a safe distance. I'll ask them what they want and we can go from there."

"You think it'll be that easy?"

"Probably not," said Max. "But if there's something we can give them that makes this all go away, it'd be preferable to fighting. We simply aren't equipped to deal with gunshot wounds. I got lucky with mine, and the next one of us that gets shot—well, I doubt they'll be so lucky."

"You're crazy, man," said Chad.

"Maybe," said Max.

Georgia knew Max well enough to know that diplomacy in a situation like this was the last place his mind would go to. Max was always willing to step up to fight when necessary. He never looked for fights, but he didn't shy away from them either, not when lives were on the line.

Georgia was turning Max's words over and over in her head. The more she thought about it, the more she actually agreed with Max. It certainly wasn't ideal, but the thought of engaging in another firefight made her feel sick to her stomach. She had images in her mind of James and Sadie getting shot and bleeding out on the ground. The last time they'd stopped to siphon gas, they'd gotten lucky. It easily could have ended horribly, with James lying dead on the ground.

"I think we should do it," said Georgia. "It's worth a shot.

If they get close, you can hop back in and we can speed off again."

"Good," said Max. "Do it up here, down this straightaway."

"You sure you want to do it now?" Georgia was thinking Max might want to think it over before acting.

"The sooner the better," said Max.

"This is nuts," said Chad. "You can't do this. They're just going to shoot you. What if they've got rifles with scopes or something?"

"For once I agree with Chad," said Mandy.

"Don't do it, Max," said Sadie. She sounded worried for Max's safety. Georgia knew that while Sadie wouldn't ever admit it, she admired Max. James did too. He'd do anything Max said.

"I'm doing it," said Max. "Unless anyone has a better plan."

No one said anything.

They were at the straightaway. There was nothing but trees on either side of the road. There wasn't a house in sight.

Georgia didn't even ask if the Bronco was still following them. She knew it would be.

Georgia slowed the minivan down. She didn't pull over to the side of the road at all, so that it'd be easier to make a getaway if they needed to. Not that the loaded-down minivan would be able to outrun the Bronco anyway. But at least if they needed to, they could get driving again. Although...

Her thoughts were going round and round with the possibilities. There were too many of them.

"I'll leave the door open," said Max, opening the sliding door, getting ready to step outside.

"Max," said Mandy, her voice barely above a whisper. "Be careful."

Georgia was watching Max. There was determination on his face. He stepped out, turned around, and nodded to everyone.

He stood there in the open air, binoculars to his eyes, watching.

"It's coming," said Max. "It looks like they're slowing down. I'm going to flag them down. Let them know I want to talk."

There was no way Georgia could think about it that ended well. It was just a question of how badly it would go.

30

JOHN

"You sure you're going to come?"

The woman nodded again.

"What's your name?"

"Cynthia."

"I'm John." There was no point with last names. At least not the way John figured it.

"We'd better get going," said John. "Unless we want to stay the day here. I only travel by night. Less of a chance of getting seen or caught or killed."

The woman just nodded. She was still crying, staring at her dead husband.

There were cars in the driveways of the neighboring houses. There must have been people still in their homes. And they must have heard the gunshots and the trucks. But they didn't leave their houses. No one came to help. They were too scared. It made John mad, even though he didn't blame them. They were protecting themselves, as best they could, looking out for themselves. He couldn't fault them for that. But his blood was boiling, and his chest felt hot with anger.

"Do you have anything in the house we could use?" said John. "I know you said they took all the food."

"I don't know."

"Come on, let's go look. Time's passing."

"What are we going to do with him?"

"With John?"

She nodded, her eyes fixed on her husband.

John knew she'd want to bury him. But there wasn't time.

"We've got to get going," said John. "I'm sorry, but there isn't time to bury him."

John walked over to a large bush, broke off a couple branches, and laid them down over the woman's husband. His face remained uncovered. John closed the eyelids one by one. The gaze of death was concealed.

The woman was muttering something to herself, probably saying a prayer.

John had to take her hand and tug her until she budged, heading back into her darkened house.

Being physically removed from her husband's body had an awakening effect on her. It was slight, but it was there. She was able to take some action now. She took a candle from a table in the pitch-black house and lit it with a match.

Together, they searched the house quickly for anything they might take. The woman had a backpack that John carried for her, leaving his own pack by the door. He filled it with things he could see by the candlelight.

The militia soldiers had torn through the house, leaving hardly anything unturned. Tables had been toppled over and doors had been broken, and for no reason at all.

There wasn't a scrap of food in the kitchen. All the kitchen knives were gone.

"Do you have a shed, a garage?"

"No."

"Any tools, anything like that? Camping gear?"

"No, we've never been into anything like that."

John sighed. There wasn't much that would be of value for them.

The best he could do was to gather all the candles that remained, the ones that the soldiers had overlooked in their hasty raid. Along with the candles, John took blankets from the beds.

Cynthia took a picture of herself and her husband. She wasn't foolish, and didn't go for jewelry or anything like that. Interestingly, the soldiers hadn't either.

John could understand taking the picture, but when she took a book from her bedside table, John had to say something in protest.

"Do you really need that?"

"I guess not."

"What is it?"

"*The Savage Detectives.*"

"A crime novel?"

"Not really. It's fiction, I guess. It means a lot to me... My husband gave it to me."

"We've got to go," said John. "Take it. Come on. We can't spend any more time here. Daylight's coming."

They left through the backyard. John wore his backpack and she wore hers. He carried his hoe, and he handed her his kitchen knife, telling her to keep it in hand at all times.

John led the way at first, and she followed. But they soon realized that she knew the area far better than he did. She'd lived there for ten years, after all, and she knew which backyards they could cut easily through and when it'd make more sense to cross the street. Or if it was better to risk walking along the sidewalk for a short distance.

A couple times they lost precious time by having to hide, frozen, in a backyard when a truck had rumbled by. A couple times they'd heard shouting. No gunfire, though.

It was getting close to dawn when they arrived at the top of the huge hill. They were both sweating and exhausted. John was ravenous and his throat was parched.

"I don't know whether to go through King of Prussia, or Valley Forge," he said.

"I used to go running at Valley Forge Park all the time," said Cynthia.

"You know it well then?"

"You could say that."

"Park it is then," said John, making the decision quickly. "But I'm worried we're not going to get there by morning."

"If we take Maple Street," said Cynthia, "we can save a lot of time. We can cut right through to the park."

"I'm starting to think it's good I brought you along."

Cynthia didn't say anything. But then again, she was still grieving. Her husband was freshly dead. And he didn't even qualify as "freshly buried."

Maple Street was a long, narrow road. Beautiful trees formed a canopy overhead. The sun was rising, and light was spreading out across the world.

The view was incredible, but John was worried. There'd be nowhere to hide in the daylight.

Twenty minutes later, they'd made it to the southeast corner of Valley Forge Park.

They crossed over a road and made their way into the park, which was, in parts, thickly forested. They crossed a single dirt trail as they headed deeper into the wilder areas of the park. Cynthia knew the way well, which was good, because John wouldn't have known which way to go. If he'd been by himself, he could have easily found himself exiting the park by mistake, or heading to the main trail and the parking lots.

For all John knew, there were people in the park. After all, it was the biggest public space in the entire area. Maybe people would have come here to camp, to get away from the power outage, thinking that they were far enough removed. John already knew better. There wasn't any escaping this madness. At least not until one was much farther away.

John was exhausted when he finally set his pack down. He lay on the ground and stared up through the trees at the slowly brightening sky. Near him, Cynthia was softly crying.

"We're going to have to hide out in the woods for the day," said John. "We can eat, and then you can rest. I'll take first shift, and then wake you up in the middle of the night."

"OK," said Cynthia, her voice soft and weak.

He knew that he had no words of comfort for her that would ring true.

"You'd better eat something," said John, groaning as he finally sat up, getting into a cross-legged position. He started rummaging through his pack for the energy bars, and handed one to Cynthia.

"Thanks."

"I've got to take a leak," said John.

He hadn't urinated since the shed, where he'd gone in the corner, leaving himself to deal with the smell for the rest of the day.

He walked a little ways away from Cynthia, heading further into the park. When he looked over his shoulder, he could still see her, sitting there, her energy bar untouched and unopened.

He undid his pants and let out a sigh of relief as the urine started to flow.

In the silence of the morning, without any nearby

freeway traffic, there was nothing but the sound of the birds and squirrels.

Or so he would have thought.

From off in the distance came the unmistakable sound of human voices.

Human voices and human laughter, mixed together.

John cut himself off midstream, in order to listen better. The sounds were faint, but they were definitely there.

If he hadn't known any better, he would have said it sounded like a party. A large one.

He turned around and motioned for Cynthia to come over. But she didn't see him gesturing.

"Cynthia," he hissed, trying to speak loudly and quietly at the same time.

She looked up.

"Come over!"

She came over, and her ears must have been a little better than John's, because she perked her ears when she was still about ten feet from John.

"You hear that?" said John.

She nodded. "Sounds like a party."

"Who would be throwing a party during a time like this?"

John already knew the answer. People that they didn't want to run into, that's who.

31

MAX

The Ford Bronco had stopped a ways down the road. One of the men had gotten out of truck and was walking slowly towards Max. He was big and burly, with a thick frame and an equally thick neck. Max couldn't yet make out his features without the binoculars, and he didn't want to raise them, since it might be seen as some gesture of aggression or trickery. The other man stayed in the Bronco.

This may have been Max's worst idea yet. But he was going to go through with it. If he'd been by himself, he would have just fought them. Even if it had meant dying. But there were the others to think about, particularly James and Sadie. They were too young to die in a gunfight.

That was all coming from Max's brain. It was all reasoning.

What was coming from his gut was something different. His gut was telling him that the men wanted something from them. They didn't necessarily want to fight to get it, but of course a threat was definitely on the table. The threat of physical violence. But the men had passed by slowly in their car. They'd had the opportunity to attack them then. They'd had the opportunity to attack them for miles and miles. But instead they'd followed at a distance. If that wasn't an indication that they wanted something, Max didn't know what was.

Max had gestured to them, waving his arms in the air in some kind of makeshift semaphore language. He hadn't been sure he'd gotten the point across, but then the man had gotten down from the Bronco and started approaching. Maybe the whole meaning hadn't gotten through, but some part of it had.

The man walking towards him was getting closer. He held a shotgun, but he didn't point it at Max. Instead, he held it casually, letting the muzzle point towards the ground.

Max had his hand on his Glock, but it stayed in its holster.

The man stopped when he was in shouting distance.

Neither spoke for what felt like a long time.

"What do you want?" shouted Max finally.

No response. At least not yet.

Max waited. He gripped his Glock tighter.

"Food?" shouted Max. "Weapons? What do you want? I'm willing to negotiate."

The man started laughing. He must have to put extra force behind it, to make it heard from where Max was standing. It was like a combination between a shout and a laugh. Max hadn't heard anything like it. Laughter projected like that was creepy. It sent a chill down Max's spine.

"We want one thing," shouted the man.

Max waited.

The man was building the suspense on purpose, it seemed.

A gust of wind blew through the trees, ruffling Max's

hair. Overhead, clouds moved across the sun, darkening the day.

"We want the women," shouted the man. "The two young ones."

He wanted the women? What the hell?

Max felt disgusted. So society had collapsed and these men were looking to kidnap themselves wives or pleasure objects? What kind of sick men was he dealing with?

Max didn't answer. There simply wasn't an answer for a demand like that.

"Give us the two," shouted the man. "And we'll leave you all alone. Trust me, you don't stand a chance against us. We're going to get what we want, one way or another. Doesn't matter to us."

"Over my dead body," shouted Max.

The man laughed again, that creepy extra-loud laugh. "With pleasure."

Max drew his Glock. But he was probably too far to get off a good shot. The man's shotgun wasn't going to be much good either. Likely, the men had other weapons in the truck. He held the shotgun with practiced casual ease, indicating that he was familiar with weapons.

Max jumped back in the van, as best he could with his leg.

"Go!" he shouted.

Georgia, of course, already had the van in drive. A second later, they were off.

Behind them, the man stood watching them, not making a move to get back into the Bronco quickly. The way he waited, unconcerned, was more concerning than his insane demand. It was as if he already knew he could get what he wanted.

"Faster," shouted Max.

Georgia didn't need to be told. The minivan was speeding down the rural road. The engine was whining, a high-pitched noise it hadn't made before. They'd never pushed the minivan to its limits, not like this.

Georgia was a good driver. She knew how to take the turns. She knew when she could push the minivan and when she couldn't.

"They're going to take us?" said Sadie.

"Sick freaks," said Chad.

"We're not going to let anything happen to you," said Georgia.

"Don't worry, Sadie. They're just some sickos," added Chad.

Mandy didn't say anything.

Max had worked his way into the back. He had his binoculars to his eyes.

"If there's a turnoff, take it," he shouted. He still hadn't lowered his volume from when he'd been shouting at the man. His heart was racing and his skin felt ice cold. These guys had scared him. There was something... professional about them... and something cold, impossibly cold.

There still wasn't any sign of them.

But Max knew they wouldn't be far behind. They were simply letting Max and the others get a head start. Maybe it was fun to them. Maybe it was just a game.

If they could just turn off somewhere, down some side road, maybe they had a chance of losing the men.

But there was no road.

It was just straight ahead, for as far as the eye could see.

"There's nowhere to turn," shouted Georgia.

Through his binoculars, Max saw the Ford Bronco appearing in the distance.

It was coming for them.

32

JOHN

John couldn't believe what he was seeing.

He and Cynthia had crawled on their bellies through the tall grasses of Valley Forge Park.

In front of them, a few hundred yards away, a few small fires burned. They were dwindling now, nothing more than small echoes of what must have been huge bonfires.

Around the fires, there were a few dozen people. Mostly in their twenties and early thirties, it seemed. Some wore normal clothes, and some were dressed in bright costumes. Some were completely nude, dancing energetically.

Many were laughing, dancing wildly. Some were making out, couples lying deep in the tall grasses. Some were passed out, sleeping right out in the open. Some were staring at the rising sun, gazes fixed.

"What the hell are they doing?" whispered John to Cynthia.

"Partying."

"Partying? What?"

"Looks like they're having a big party."

"Don't they know what's happened?"

John kept carefully studying the partiers. He was so used to death and violence now that the scene before him seemed completely inconceivable. He scanned the ground, looking for any sign of weapons, for any sign of violence. But there wasn't any.

There were coolers here and there. A couple grills sat near the fires. They'd gone to the trouble of carting grills all the way out here?

John's mind simply couldn't make sense of what he was seeing.

"Hey!" shouted someone.

Shit, they'd seen John or Cynthia.

"Hey, look! Newcomers!"

A woman in her twenties had stopped dancing. She was pointing and waving at John and Cynthia. There was a huge smile on her face.

John didn't know what to feel. He felt fear, and felt silly for feeling scared.

The woman was wearing a bikini and nothing else. Her long blonde hair hung down around her chest. She was deeply tanned and all smiles. None of the other revelers seemed to pay attention to her.

She jogged over to where John and Cynthia lay hidden, moving jauntily.

"Hey!" she said, stopping in front of them, putting her hands on her hips. "What are you two doing down there?"

"Uh," said John.

He'd been through so much. This seemed too strange. This young woman seemed like she was living in a different world entirely. She was acting like she was at a beach party, and that society had never collapsed.

"Hiding," said Cynthia.

"Well come on, there's no need to hide. Join the party!"

John finally stood up. He was about a head taller than the young woman.

"The party?" said John. "What party?" It was a dumb thing to say, but he was too flabbergasted to say anything else.

"The party!" she said, bouncing up and down with excitement as she spoke. She gestured over to the dozens of others. "Right over there! It's one of the best. You've got to come. We're having so much fun."

John saw that the woman's pupils were dilated. She was on something. Maybe ecstasy, judging by the way she was acting.

"Don't you realize what's happened?" said John.

"What do you mean?" She spoke with a high-pitched, innocent voice, full of wonder and enthusiasm. Not to mention complete denial about the world's situation.

"Everything's... gone to shit," said John. "Society's collapsing..." He didn't even know where to begin.

"They killed my husband," said Cynthia.

"A rogue militia has overtaken the Main Line," said John. "The city... it's complete chaos..."

"You've got to look on the positive side," said the young woman. She wouldn't stop bouncing.

John's jaw fell open. He couldn't believe what he was hearing. So she definitely knew what was happening, but was choosing to live in extreme denial.

"We came out here to party when the power went out," she said. "And we're having the best time of our lives."

"Aren't you worried?" said John.

"Worried? What for?"

"Do you have food?"

"Food? We ran out of it a week ago or so. We've got plenty of molly, though."

John knew that molly was a term for high quality MDMA, or ecstasy. He'd taken some once, after a night of drinking, and he'd woken up the next day with the worst headache of his life, unable to read his financial spreadsheets at work, his mouth and throat parched beyond belief.

The pills would keep them happy, maybe, but it wouldn't feed them or keep them alive.

"Come on," said John, taking Cynthia's arm. "We've got to go."

"You're leaving? You're not going to party with us? We've got plenty of molly for everyone."

John knew there was nothing he could say that could convince the young woman or her friends of anything. They'd chosen to tackle the collapse of modern civilization with pure hedonism and nothing more.

John led Cynthia away from the party, back to their packs in the woods. The young woman called out to them the whole way, urging them to come back to party.

"They're not going to last long," said Cynthia, taking a long drink of water and opening an energy bar.

"No," said John, shaking his head. "No, they're not. I'm surprised nothing's happened to them yet."

"I guess they have nothing the militia would want to steal."

"Maybe," said John, shaking his head in disbelief. "I'm dead tired, and I bet you are too. Let's get some rest."

"I'll take the first watch," said Cynthia. "I'll wake you up in the afternoon. We'll leave after dark, right?"

"Right," said John. "Thanks."

Cynthia sat cross-legged, eating her energy bar. There

were tears in her eyes as she looked towards the distance where the partiers were.

John lay down in his clothes, using one of Cynthia's blankets as a make-shift pillow. He was so tired he'd be asleep in seconds. As he closed his eyes, he wondered if it was really wise to put his trust and life in the hands of a woman he'd just met. He doubted she'd betray him, but what if she decided to leave him sleeping there, completely unprotected? John didn't wonder long. He was asleep within moments, too exhausted to worry any longer.

33

MAX

Max's heart was pounding in his chest.

There was no turnoff ahead. There was no chance to lose them.

Max knew there was only one thing to do. And that was fight.

His mind was fixed. He was determined. He only saw one way out. And he wouldn't change his mind, no matter what. Even if it meant sacrificing himself.

He didn't know why he'd decided on what he had. He didn't know why he was so dedicated to saving these people that he hadn't even known a couple weeks ago. Maybe it was because he hadn't had a purpose in his pre-EMP life. He'd just been an office drone, longing for a purpose, longing for some way to give his life meaning.

Now he had a purpose. Now his life could have meaning.

But it might mean losing his life in the process.

Max was OK with that.

He felt alive, like he never had before. Intense energy filled him, drowning out the pain.

"All right," said Max, speaking loudly, his voice sounding

commanding as it boomed through the minivan interior. "Here's what we're going to do. And it's not up for discussion. Georgia, you're going to slow down and I'll drive. I'll drop you all off, and then I'll lead them down the road, away from you. You're going to take with you what you can and run into the woods. Don't turn back."

"You can't do this, Max," said Mandy.

"I'm doing it," said Max. "No arguing."

"You don't stand a chance against them alone, Max," said Georgia. "I'm going with you."

Max considered it.

Georgia had every reason to stay with him. She knew, as well as he did, that Sadie and Mandy had a better chance of avoiding capture if the men in the Bronco died. If Max went alone, and died without killing them, they'd still be on the hunt. They'd be more energized than before, more willing to do whatever it took to get what they'd wanted all along. Sure, it would give Sadie and Mandy a head start, but how far could they really get on foot?

The best case scenario would be if Max could stay behind to fight, letting them continue on in the van. But there wasn't a situation where that would be possible.

"OK," said Max. "Georgia and I will go in the van. Everyone else, we're going to drop you off, and you're going to run."

"This is crazy," said Mandy.

"It's the only way," said Max.

"I'm staying too," said James.

"You're going to stay with your sister, James," said Georgia. There was finality in her tone. James knew enough not to argue. "She's going to need someone to protect her."

"I'll stay then," said Chad.

"It's better if you go, Chad," said Max. "You can protect them. James and Sadie are just kids. Sorry, James."

"I'm not letting you two stay to die," said Mandy.

"Who said anything about dying?" said Max. But he knew in his heart that the chances of him and Georgia surviving this were slim. But at least with the two of them, they'd most likely be able to kill the Bronco men too. They'd go down fighting.

"What goes for Chad goes for you too, Mandy," said Max.

"Where should I pull over, Max?" said Georgia.

"Next curve," said Max.

The atmosphere in the minivan was frantic.

"Mom, you can't do this," Sadie said.

"Take good care of her, James," said Georgia. It sounded like she was trying to keep her voice steady, trying to keep herself from crying.

"Take food and guns with you," said Max. "And water. Nothing else."

They weren't moving to get ready. They were stunned from Max's plan.

"Come on!" shouted Max. "Get a move on it! When we pull over, you're getting out. You're only going to have thirty seconds to clear the van and get into the woods to cover. If they see you, the plan is over."

That got them moving, scrambling around.

Max's tactic was to shock them into movement, to get them to do something that they didn't want to do, but something that would save their lives.

"Everyone ready?" said Max.

James knew the deal. He had sprung into action, and was moving around the van, distributing things.

"We're close to the Ohio border," said Max. "There's a

little town on the other side of 90, in Pennsylvania, called Albion. Head there. If we make it, we'll meet you there, at the old granary outside on the edge of town."

Albion was the only place Max could think of. He'd been there once, long ago, as a kid on a trip with his parents and his brother. He remembered that old granary for some reason.

Albion was as good of a place as any to meet. It was close to the big interstate, which would be easier to find than any other landmark. If they all lived, they could continue on over the border to Ohio.

"If you make it?" said Sadie. She was crying.

"Come on, Sadie," said James. "We've got to get ready."

"We can't leave Mom and Max."

"It's going to be OK, Sadie. Everything's going to be fine," said James.

The minivan had just rounded the corner. The Bronco wasn't in sight.

"Now!" shouted Max.

Georgia slammed on the brakes. The van jolted to an unpleasantly harsh stop.

"Go!" shouted Max.

James got the door open and was moving everyone out. He had to tug Sadie to get her out.

"Take care of them," said Max, speaking to no one in particular. They were all responsible for each other.

They all had their rifles in their hands. They had some food with them. Just a little bit. It'd have to be enough. They had water. They'd make it. Max knew it.

Georgia already had her foot on the gas. They were moving. Fast. Max slammed the sliding door closed.

It was just Georgia and Max now. It was all up to them.

James, Sadie, and Chad had already disappeared into

the trees, out of view. Mandy was partially visible. Max looked at her through the rear window of the minivan. He couldn't tell, but it seemed as if she was looking at him. Then she disappeared.

Good, thought Max. They were out of sight.

They were barreling down a straightaway. Behind them, the Ford Bronco appeared.

"They're back," said Max. "Everyone got away safely."

"So what's the plan?" said Georgia, from the driver's seat.

"We're going to have to wing it."

"You know you don't have to do this, right, Max?"

"I know," said Max.

He was watching the Bronco through his binoculars. The plan seemed to have worked. They hadn't spotted the minivan stopping.

"We'd better lead them a little farther down," said Max. "Give Mandy and everyone a chance to get a move on it."

He noticed that he'd said Mandy's name and no one else's. But there wasn't time to wonder about what that meant.

Georgia drove fast along the tree-lined rural road.

Max was busy getting himself ready. He checked to make sure he had his knife and his flashlight. He tightened the laces on his boots. He checked his Glock and his rifle.

"You have any family, Max?" said Georgia.

It seemed like a strange question, considering the situation. But she must have been thinking about James and Sadie, and what would happen to them if something happened to her.

"A brother," said Max. "Estranged, though, I guess you could say."

Georgia didn't say anything.

An idea suddenly came to Max. His mind was racing

with possibilities, but only one seemed like it would work well.

He was going to have to get underhanded. He was going to have to fight dirty if he wanted to survive. That was OK. This wasn't the time for honor or principles. This was the time for staying alive, at whatever cost.

"These guys are in it for the fun," said Max. "I'm going to give them what they want. Pull the van over."

"Pull over? Are you sure?"

"Yeah," said Max. "I'm going to challenge them to a fight. Man to man. Hand to hand."

"Why would they do that? They could just shoot us. It'd be easier."

"I'll tell them that if they win and kill me, you'll tell them where the girls are. Plus, they're going to like this. If I read them right, they're in it for the chase, for the adventures. They're sickos. This'll be right up their alley. Killing a man in hand to hand combat isn't something most relish. It's despicable. But these guys, I can see it in his eyes, this is what he's been waiting for. He won't pass up a chance like this."

Georgia slowed the van down, eventually stopping.

In the pack taken from the farmhouse attackers, Max took a Ka-Bar combat knife and its sheath. It was a thin sheath, and Max was able to stuff it into the laces of his boot. He made sure his pant leg covered the boot, making the knife invisible.

"We're going to play dirty," said Max. "I want you to be ready with your rifle. Don't hesitate to shoot if the moment's right."

"I can't get them both," said Georgia. "I'll be able to take one out, and the other one will kill you."

"Wait until the moment's right then," said Max. "And don't let them see the rifle."

Max slid open the minivan door.

"Max," said Georgia.

"Yeah?"

"Thanks."

Max gave her a stiff nod and stepped out onto the road.

The wind had picked up, ruffling his hair and his shirt. His hair had grown longer than he normally let it. There hadn't been time since the EMP to worry about keeping up appearances. The stubble on his face was thick.

Max had his Glock in its holster. He didn't reach for it. He raised his hands in the air and began limping towards the Ford Bronco, which was slowing to a stop some hundred meters behind the minivan.

The men sat in the Bronco for just a moment, before the passenger got out.

He looked bigger, somehow, than he had before. Beefy and strong, like he'd spent his whole life eating and working out, trying to get as big as possible. He must have been eating pretty well since the EMP.

Max, on the other hand, had lost weight since the EMP, as everyone in his group had. But he was still strong, a wiry sort of natural strength that came from somewhere inside him.

Max kept his hands in the air, even though the other man had his shotgun with him as before.

"What's all this?" shouted the man.

Max kept walking towards him, closing the distance. He saw the man looking towards the van.

"Where are the others?"

"They're gone," said Max.

The man kept peering at the van.

"There's still one there. This is your plan or something?" The man spoke with a gruff voice, full of sickness and cruelty. "You thought you could let them escape and fight us yourself?"

"Something like that," said Max.

"We can still have fun with that one in the van," said the man. "She'll do just fine, and then we'll find the others. Don't worry. We know these woods like the backs of our hands."

"I've got a proposition for you," said Max.

"Yeah?" said the man, spitting a glob of tobacco onto the ground.

Max had never been a smoker or dipper, but he'd tried dip once in high school. He remembered the pleasant buzz, the rush of energy. It could be useful for a situation like this, but Max knew that he didn't need it. The adrenaline was enough for him. He felt like he could handle anything.

"Hand to hand combat," said Max. "One on one. We fight like men. To the death. If you win, my partner there will tell you where the girls are."

The man studied Max in silence. He started laughing, that same laugh as before.

The wind blew in gusts. Dead leaves from the year before danced across the two lanes of blacktop.

"Sounds like fun," said the man.

Max almost breathed a sigh of relief. He'd accepted the deal. The plan had worked. So far.

The hardest part was yet to come.

"If you pull any tricks," said the man. "My partner's got a high powered rifle with a scope. You don't want to mess with him."

Max knew that even if he won, the man's partner wouldn't hesitate to pull the trigger. Max knew that these men had no honor. And that was why he wasn't going to play by the rules either. He just hoped Georgia was faster than the other one.

The man walked back to the Ford, keeping himself facing Max the whole time. He had a few words with his partner in the Bronco.

"It's a deal," he shouted.

He lay his shotgun on the hood of the Bronco.

"Leave that Glock, though."

Max removed the Glock from its holster and set it down on the road.

"You armed?" said Max.

"Of course."

The man took a Glock of his own from a holster. And he took a revolver out too. He set both down.

The other man in the Bronco stepped out. He held a high-powered rifle in his hands. He pointed it at the van.

A shot rang out, intensely loud.

Max hadn't been hit. He looked back at the van. One of the tires had been shot out.

Another shot. Another tire had been hit, completely deflated.

The back of the minivan sunk towards the ground, both its rear tires punctured. Georgia wouldn't get far in the van like that.

The men both grinned and laughed.

"That's so your partner doesn't try to escape when I finish you off."

Georgia would have no way to escape. Max would have to kill them. And Georgia would have to shoot the other. There wasn't any other way out.

He and Max approached each other.

Max knew that it was a good bet that a guy who carried

two large handguns had other sorts of weapons on him. But he didn't ask. He had his own knife on him, and he wasn't going to set those down. He was expecting trickery from the man, a knife pulled on him when he was least expecting it. Max knew he'd have to act first.

The man spat on the ground again, while looking Max directly in the eyes.

They were close now. Only ten feet from each other.

The man's face was full of small scars. A large scar ran down his neck. He'd been in fights before, bad ones.

He was at least a full head taller than Max.

No words were spoken.

They stared into each other's eyes. The man didn't blink.

Suddenly, he let out a yell, an animal-like growl, and charged Max. His head was low, his body lurching forward.

Max stepped to the side, but not fast enough. His injured leg slowed him down.

The man collided with Max, knocking him to the ground.

Max's lungs were deflated. He struggled to breathe.

The man rolled on top of him. He was heavy, his weight pressing down on Max. He raised his arm and swung down, expertly shifting the weight of his torso to add more power to the punch. His fist was hard and it connected with the side of Max's face.

Max felt dizzy. The pain seared through him.

Another punch, this one in his stomach. Though not as hard.

Max finally got in one of his own, sending his fist smashing into the man's face.

The man got up and stood over Max, laughing.

"Nice one," he said. "I was worried for a second this was going to be too easy. I want to have some fun."

Good, thought Max. Let his opponent not take it too seriously. Let him think it's a game. Let him have his fun. Until the moment is right and he dies.

Max wanted as many chances as he could get. He didn't care that the man was giving him a breather, just to toy with him more. It'd be better for Max in the end.

"You fight OK," said the man. "But you don't stand a chance against me. Come on, get up."

Max struggled to his feet. His leg was killing him.

They both put their hands up, and began slowly circling each other. Each was looking for the chance to get a punch in.

The man came at Max with a right hook, fast and powerful.

Max managed to dodge it, even with his leg, stepping to the side.

He came back at his opponent with a left hook, even though he was right handed. It caught the man in the side, and he lost his breath for a moment before straightening back up.

"Good one," he said. "But you've got to hit me harder than that."

The continued circling each other, punching and dodging. The wind was blowing and time was passing.

Max took another punch, this one to the face. Blood streamed out from his nose. It might have been broken. Not that it mattered.

He'd gotten the man in the stomach with an uppercut, but the man was strong, and he didn't seem winded at all.

"I'm getting tired of this," said the man, spitting. "You're stronger than I thought. But not as fun."

Max said nothing. He kept his thoughts to himself.

"You haven't said a damn word," said the man. "You're

too good or something? Is that it? Taking the high road? I'll show you the high road."

The man reached into his pocket and drew forth a folding knife. It was an automatic, and a second later, with the push of a button, a vicious looking double-edged dagger blade shot forth from the handle.

The man charged Max, holding the knife, ready to stab.

Max dodged the blade, but he couldn't dodge the man's bulk.

The man collided with Max and they both fell to the ground.

Max was on his back, looking up into the man's gruesome, scarred face. Max's body was pinned down, under the man's massive weight.

Before the man could stab him, Max seized the man's knife hand with both of his own. He twisted, pulling down, hard. But he still didn't let go of the knife.

Max let go with one hand and swung with a close fist at the knife. Part of his fist landed on the knife blade, cutting Max's hand. But he'd hit the handle too, and the knife went flying, clattering on the pavement.

Max bent his leg, bringing his boot closer to his hand. He was reaching for the knife in his boot. This was his chance.

"Don't think I don't know about the knife in your boot," snarled the man. His hand slammed down on Max's hand, pinning his wrist against the pavement. "Oldest trick in the book."

Max's other hand was free. And bleeding.

He dug into his pocket, his fingers closing around his folding knife. His thumb found the hole. He opened the blade in his pocket.

"I'll just beat you to death," spat the man. His eyes were

glowing with rage. "This is for trying to stab me... a damn dirty trick..."

His fist collided with Max's face.

Max saw stars. His vision went blurry.

Max saw the fist rising again, ready to strike. One more blow and Max knew he'd be unconscious.

Max drew the knife from his pocket with his left hand. He brought it up fast, drawing it across the man's throat, slicing diagonally.

A line of blood appeared on his throat.

Everything seemed to pause. Blood started gushing, flowing freely from the long cut.

A garbled, messy scream, muted.

The man was gasping for breath. It sounded like he was underwater. Blood-filled coughs.

Max felt the hot blood splatter onto his own face.

Thirty seconds later, the man was dead. His heavy weight collapsed fully onto Max. Max pushed, but he couldn't get out from underneath the corpse.

Max could barely see.

He could only think of one thing... Georgia.

Two shots rang out. Like a syncopated rhythm. One after the other. Rapid and loud.

Georgia had shot her rifle. The other man had shot his.

Who had lived? Had either of them?

34

JOHN

It had been many days since John and Cynthia had left Valley Forge Park. They'd walked north during the dark nights and slept during the days. The journey was exhausting, and they were hungry and often incredibly thirsty. They had to ration the energy bars, since it was the only food they had. They'd gone through phases of being completely sickened by the flavor of the bars to enjoying them again, and then the cycle repeated itself. In the end, they didn't have a choice. They were the only things available to eat.

It had been tempting, when they'd reached dawn, to simply abandon the watch system, letting both of them sleep at the same time. In the end, though, keeping watch had saved their lives at least once. Cynthia had been awake when a group of men and women had come through the forest. John and Cynthia never learned who they were or what, if anything, they were looking for, because Cynthia had shaken John awake and they'd rushed off silently through the woods.

John and Cynthia had stayed away from the road as much

as they could. They walked in a single file line, Cynthia staying about fifteen feet behind John. They didn't get a chance to talk much that way, which was OK, since there wasn't much to talk about. At the end of a long night of walking, they were both too tired to chitchat. And it didn't feel appropriate, anyway, with society crumbling all around them. They'd settled into a comfortable, strange little routine.

John was left with his own thoughts most of the time. But he found that he didn't have many of them. After everything he'd been through, and with the exhaustion, his mind seemed to want to rest. His dreams, though, were filled with chaos and violence. The images haunted him for the first few hours of waking. Then, he was able to shake them off and let his mind be free of everything, nothing but a blank slate. In many ways, the terrain seemed to calm him on its own. He remembered hearing that people actually became more relaxed when out in nature, compared to living in cities. Maybe something like that was happening to him. He didn't know, and he didn't think much about it.

John had lost track of how many days they'd been walking for. Maybe close to a month. He didn't know. He hoped that they were close to the farmhouse by now. He hoped that they were headed in the right direction. They were going completely off the North Star. But just going north obviously wasn't going to be good enough. They could have easily passed by the farmhouse by a few miles and they never would have known.

It was getting close to morning. The light was starting to come up. Earlier in their journey, they'd been careful to never walk when there was any light. But now that they hadn't run into a single soul in many, many miles, they had gotten a little more relaxed. John was also interested in making good time, and the more minutes they spent walking each day, the closer he figured they'd be to the farmhouse.

There was something up ahead. Something metallic between the trees. John couldn't make out what it was, but he saw the early morning light flashing off of whatever it was.

He stopped in his tracks, and waited for Cynthia to catch up to him.

"Do you see that?" he said. He wasn't going to rule out the possibility that he was suffering hallucinations from exhaustion and hunger.

"Yeah," said Cynthia. "I see it."

It might have been the first time they'd talked in days. John wasn't sure.

"Do you know what it is?"

"I don't know," said Cynthia.

"We'd better go around it."

"There's no movement."

"Yeah, but who knows what it is."

"Let's go a little closer."

John knew why she was saying this. Even though they were safe, they were becoming stimuli-starved. The woods looked the same day in and day out, and they simply hadn't seen anything resembling civilization in a long time. Something metallic and shiny and large was bound to be interesting.

"OK," said John.

He was feeling despondent, possibly, and more willing to take a risk. After all, maybe they'd never find the farmhouse. And their supplies wouldn't last forever. What would they do after that?

He and Cynthia broke tradition by walking side by side through the woods, towards the metallic glinting.

The object was bigger than they'd thought. It seemed to stretch forever.

As they got closer, John suddenly realized what it was.

Cynthia had the same realization. At the same time.

"Shit," muttered John.

Cynthia covered her mouth with her hands in horror and surprise.

It was a commercial airplane, crashed in the Pennsylvania woods. It was a big plane, the type that carried hundreds of people, but John didn't know what the model number would have been.

There was no movement. There didn't seem to be anyone there.

John doubted there'd be survivors. He scanned the area near the plane, and saw bits of the wreckage scattered among the trees in a line for miles. Trees had toppled over, shattered and broken.

The closer they got, the more horrific the crash appeared to be. There was simply no way there were survivors.

"They must have lost power during the EMP," said John. "This is an old crash. Must have happened weeks ago."

The cabin of the plane was torn completely open, revealing a scattering of decomposing bodies, victims of the crash.

John didn't know what to think or feel. He'd seen so much death already. But this was... it was different, somehow.

Cynthia had tears in her eyes as she looked at the bodies.

"Come on," said John. "We've got to see if there's any food."

"I... can't..." said Cynthia.

"Come on," said John. "I know you can do it. You want to live just as much as I do."

The truth was, his desire to live spiked and plummeted constantly, and he never knew quite where he stood anymore.

Whatever fires had burned here had long gone out, leaving scattered and charred remains of things long past the point of recognition.

John and Cynthia walked through the wreckage, through the bodies, hunting down packets of airplane food that might have survived.

They spent three hours in the rising sun looking for food. They came away from the carcass of the aircraft sweating with exertion, the images of burned and torn apart bodies fresh in their minds. Miraculously, some of the airplane food had somehow survived. Maybe 20 meals or so, and pieces here and there of other meals. Some of the prepackaged meals had been torn apart, the food exposed to the air, but John took these anyway.

"About a week's worth of extra food," said John, flopping down onto the ground between two large pine trees, well away from the aircraft.

Cynthia didn't say anything.

They both fell asleep without even getting out their blankets, completely forgetting their watch system.

John woke up when the sun was going down. His body had gotten used to this odd sleeping schedule.

"Shit," he muttered, seeing Cynthia asleep as well.

He shook her awake.

"What?" she said groggily.

"We forgot to do watches," said John.

"Well, we're still alive, aren't we?"

That was all that was said about it.

They ate in silence. John relished the airplane food. It may not have been good, and some of it may have been partially rotten, but at least it wasn't another damn energy bar.

"You're not going to eat the airplane food?" said John, watching Cynthia biting into yet another energy bar.

"I can't," she said. "Not without thinking about those bodies."

"Well, you'll get hungry soon enough," said John. "We don't have a lot of these bars left."

They got up and started walking, heading north.

They were both tired and impossibly weary. The long journey had taken a toll on them. They stopped walking single file and began meandering through the woods, losing a lot of the discipline that John had insisted upon for the earlier part of the journey.

"I don't think we're ever going to find it," said John.

"Find what?"

"The farmhouse," said John.

"Oh," said Cynthia, as if she'd forgotten the point of the whole trip.

"At least," said John. "We've gotten pretty far away from everything. We're safe from the militia out here."

"Yeah," said Cynthia.

She had never really gotten over her husband's death, it seemed, and continued to carry the sadness with her.

"Wait," said John, pointing ahead. "Do you see that?"

"What?"

"That big old tree there."

"Yeah. So?"

"I... I remember that tree... Max and I used to go out there and climb up its old gnarled branches..."

When they reached the tree, John stepped closer to examine it. Sure enough, it was the tree. It was unmistakable, with its huge, knotty branches and permanently-wilted looking leaves. Whatever type of tree it was, it was ancient.

"We're close to the farmhouse," said John. He could feel the excitement building up inside of him. "We're close! Shit, I can't believe it. After all that... all those mistakes... I thought we'd missed it by miles for sure."

"You sure this is the tree?" said Cynthia.

"Dead sure."

"So we're close to your brother? The one who's super prepared and everything?"

A smile was starting to grow across Cynthia's face. It was the first time John had ever seen her smile.

"We're very close," said John. "It's just down this way. Come on."

John was excited to see the brother that he'd barely spoken to in a decade. He was excited to find a home, to feel safe. Maybe he could become useful at the farmhouse, maybe he'd feel like he belonged. It would be their safe haven, a place to escape from the horrors of what the world had become.

"There it is," said John, leading Cynthia out of the woods and into the field.

The farmhouse stood there in front of them, illuminated in the moonlight, looking more or less how it always had. John almost couldn't believe his eyes. He couldn't believe that after all that, he'd finally arrived.

"I don't see anyone," said Cynthia.

"They're probably inside," said John.

"Don't you think they'd have someone on watch?"

"Uh, I guess," said John. It did seem a little strange to him. "But maybe they're on the other side of the house or something. Or hidden. I mean, knowing Max, he'd have it all set up perfectly... everything would be just right."

John suddenly had to confront an idea that he'd been avoiding since he'd left his apartment in Philly. The fact was that John didn't actually know if Max had gotten to the farmhouse. It simply seemed like the most logical thing that could have happened. And if John had survived, how would it even be possible that Max, who was certainly going to have been wildly prepared, wouldn't have survived? It was a sobering thought, and John pushed it aside yet again.

"Come on," said John.

Together, they walked across the field and up the steps to the old porch at the front of the farmhouse.

"I don't hear anyone," said Cynthia.

"Uh, maybe they're out hunting or something," said John. "Or looking for edible plants. I'm sure Max knows all about that stuff..."

"Why do you think he has others with him? Maybe it's just him."

"Uh, I don't know. I just kind of figured... it would make more sense with more people. Max is pretty strategic. But yeah, he can be kind of a loner too... Maybe you're right, maybe it's just him by himself here. Maybe he's hiding out. Maybe he saw us approaching and didn't recognize us or something. He'll be glad to have us here. We can help him defend the house... We can start growing crops..."

John was trying so hard to believe that, against all odds, Max was here, that he was growing almost delirious with artificial excitement about all the possibilities. The facts were that no one seemed to be there.

"Max!" cried John, knocking loudly on the wood door. "Max! It's me, John, your brother. Your long lost brother! Come out from wherever you're hiding."

No one answered.

"I don't think anyone's here," said Cynthia, putting her hand on John's shoulder.

"No," said John. "He's got to be here. He's just got to be."

John lit one of the candles from Cynthia's house, holding it aloft in front of him.

The door was unlocked and John pushed it and went inside.

In the flickering candlelight, John saw a body on the floor, lying face down.

John gasped.

"Is it your brother?" said Cynthia, her voice quiet.

John bent down to examine the body. He turned the stiff body, grunting with exertion, until the lifeless face turned towards him.

"No," he said, shaking his head.

They moved through the house, finding a total of ten bodies, none of them Max.

"It looks like there was a huge battle here," said Cynthia.

She was probably right. There were bullet holes in the walls and there was blood on the floor. Not to mention the ten corpses, stiff and already stinking.

"I'm guessing there were two groups, fighting for control of the house," said John.

"Makes sense, from what I can see," said Cynthia.

They moved from room to room. In the upstairs, there were no bodies.

"This is the bedroom Max and I stayed in once when we were kids," said John, gesturing to an open door.

Inside, there was an unmade bed. On the bedside table, there was a book on a nightstand, lying halfway open, spine up. It was a book on edible plants in Pennsylvania.

John picked up the book and flipped through it. There

were notes in the margins, and the handwriting was unmistakably Max's.

"It's Max's handwriting," said John.

"Look at this," said Cynthia, flipping through a cheap notebook she'd taken from the bed. "It's some kind of journal."

John took it from her and opened it. There weren't many entries, and they weren't dated. It was unmistakably Max's handwriting, the same adult-like writing he'd used even as a child.

"Worried that people will be coming from the cities," read the first entry. "We have someone on watch at all times. But we may have to abandon the farmhouse and head to more rural areas. Lower population density means lower risk."

Below the entry, there was a rudimentary plan on how Max and his group might escape. He made mention of various people that John had never heard of, names like Mandy and Georgia. At the bottom, though, the name "Chad" appeared.

"Chad?" muttered John. "Chad Hofstetter? No, it couldn't be..." John remembered Chad well from childhood, the guy who'd never had it together and was never going to get it together. Last John had heard, Chad was still partying hard and working odd jobs to pay for his drugs, selling his blood plasma when he couldn't come up with the money for his next fix.

"Sounds like your brother is still alive," said Cynthia.

"Maybe," said John. "Sounds like he got out. But what are we going to do?"

"We could stay here."

"Stay here, and wait for more people to come, ones like

the dead men in the hallways and living room? We don't even have any guns."

"We could try," said Cynthia.

John sat down heavily on the bed.

"I guess so," he said, looking around the room that was so similar to his memory. So similar and yet the situation was so different. Society had collapsed. Who would have thought that he'd be back here decades later, wondering if he'd survive the next day?

"There *are* guns," said Cynthia. "Didn't you see all the guns those dead men have? There are dozens of them. We could use them to defend this place. We could even hunt animals... We'll do watch shifts, just like when we were hiking..."

She seemed to think it could work. John wasn't so sure.

"I guess," he said. "I mean, I'm tired of walking. I'm tired of running..."

"There's food here, too," said Cynthia. "I mean, there must be. Those guys have gear. Didn't you see their packs? Probably stuffed to the gills with food."

John didn't know why, but he started laughing. It just seemed to crazy to him that Cynthia sounded excited about the food in some dead men's packs. Then again, he'd shared a similar feeling when examining the crashed aircraft.

John let himself fall back onto the bed. His knees hung over the mattress, and the tips of his shoes barely touched the hardwood floor.

He kept laughing, laughing at the situation, laughing at the world, laughing at everything.

To John's surprise, Cynthia lay herself down on the bed. She turned on her side and pushed herself up against John. She buried her head in the crook of his arm and laughed along with him.

35

SADIE

Sadie's tears had been slow to stop.

She remembered James pulling her, practically dragging her, away from the van and into the woods.

The four of them had sprinted through the trees. The branches had smacked into them, cutting them.

They'd run and run, and Sadie had cried the entire time. She couldn't believe that her mom and Max had done what they'd done. Sadie had protested, but no one had listened. And she couldn't believe that James had gone along with the plan.

Chad had led the way, followed by James and Sadie. Sadie'd never seen Chad run so fast. Mandy took up the rear, shouting words of encouragement, telling them to keep going, to keep running.

They'd all run until they couldn't run any more, until their feet ached and their hearts pounded, feeling like they'd give out, until their lungs ached for air.

And they hadn't stopped to rest. Chad had urged them forward, telling them they had to at least walk.

There was no way to know what had happened to her

mom and Max. Sadie remembered hearing the van speeding away, the door slamming. But that was it. By the time the Bronco drove by, that evil, vicious looking SUV, Sadie and the others were too deep into the woods to hear it.

No one spoke as they walked through the woods for hours and hours. The hours turned into a full day. They'd seen nothing and no one, nothing except the endless trees.

Memories of her former life flashed through Sadie's mind as she walked. She remembered the times that her mother had wanted to take her hunting, but Sadie had been more interested in watching TV and texting her friends. She remembered how she'd never wanted to go to school, to sit in those boring classrooms and listen to someone tell her stuff she either already knew or didn't need to know. How she longed for a classroom now! Those climate-controlled rooms, once so bland and stark, couldn't have seemed more appealing compared to the forest, the horrible forest that seemed to stretch forever, terrible and vicious in its own way. And those chairs! The straight-backed chairs permanently fixed to those tiny, obnoxious desks. What Sadie wouldn't have given to have one with her right now...

Sadie felt guilty about even thinking about comfort when her mother was most likely dead. But she couldn't cry any more. It felt like her eyes had no more tears to give.

"Sadie," said James, tugging on her sleeve.

"What?"

"Didn't you hear Chad and Mandy? We're stopping for the night."

"Oh," said Sadie.

She felt dazed, lost in the strange world of her own thoughts.

"We can't start a fire," said Chad. "It's too risky."

"Here," said Mandy, putting her arm around Sadie and

handing her a bag of beef jerky. "Eat some of this. It'll make you feel better."

"I'm not hungry," said Sadie, which was the truth.

But Mandy and everyone else urged her to eat, and she did feel better afterwards.

The night was long. Impossibly long. They had nothing to sleep in. No sleeping bags, and the ground was cold. Summer was approaching its end, and the cold weather would be coming in soon.

"James?" whispered Sadie, curled up in the darkness. "Are you awake?"

"Yeah."

"You think Mom's OK?"

Sadie didn't know why she asked. She was already convinced that her mother and Max were both dead, and that the men in the Bronco would be coming for them soon.

"Yeah," said James. "You know Mom, she's tough. And Max, you can't get anything by that guy."

"Thanks," said Sadie. She suddenly realized that she'd asked because she was looking for comforting words, even if she knew in her heart that they were wrong.

The group barely spoke in the morning, except for a brief discussion about whether they were on the right track to get to Albion, the small town that Max had mentioned.

Sadie didn't get the sense that any of them actually thought there was a good chance of meeting Georgia and Max at Albion. But they all knew that they had to at least try.

After another few hours of hiking, in what Chad insisted was the wrong direction, they found Route 90, a huge, empty highway. The woods just miraculously ended. Sadie had never been so happy to see a highway in her life. It meant an end to the endless woods.

But she knew it didn't mean an end to their suffering, to the horrors they'd already experienced, and would continue to experience.

It wasn't true happiness she felt. More like the briefest of respites, like a single breath after laps and laps swimming underwater, only to be submerged once more, with nothing to do but swim and swim forever, hoping for that next brief breath of air.

"Come on, Sadie," said James.

Sadie looked up. It'd been like she was lost in a dream. Chad was already halfway across the highway.

James and Sadie crossed the highway, Mandy trailing behind them, her rifle held in front of her, ready.

It was strange to look down each way on the highway and see absolutely nothing at all. Not a single car. Not even an abandoned one.

Albion was a small town on the other side of the highway. It took them another half hour to reach the edge of it.

Sure enough, there was a rusted out old granary there, just like Max had said there would be.

But there was no Max. Her mom wasn't there either. No sign of the minivan. Or the Ford Bronco.

Sadie shuddered when she thought of that Bronco.

"Seems like no one's here," said Chad, looking up and down the abandoned dirt road. "The town must be really small. We can stay here for a while without much of a risk. What do you think, Mandy?"

"Let's wait," said Mandy.

There was an area off to the side of the granary, where overgrown hedges and trees would partially shield them all from prying eyes, if someone did come by this way.

The hours ticked by. The sun had already risen high in the sky and was headed down again.

Sadie couldn't stand the waiting. She wanted to just know. One way or the other. She wanted to know what had happened. She was trying not to hold out hope that her mom and Max had lived. But now that they were there at the meeting place, she couldn't contain the hope, and it seemed to burst through her, taking over her whole being. She'd become nothing but hope, a ridiculous and impossible hope that she knew she shouldn't even be daring to experience.

"You hear that?" said Mandy, perking up her head.

Sadie heard it. It was the sound of an engine off in the distance.

No one spoke. Everyone listened.

"It doesn't sound like the minivan," whispered James finally, as the engine noise got closer and closer.

Sadie knew he was right. It sounded louder, rougher. The minivan had either been quiet or high-pitched and whiny.

Whatever it was, whoever it was, they were getting closer every minute.

"Look," said James, pointing.

In the distance, there it was.

Unmistakable.

It was the Ford Bronco.

Coming right towards them down the road.

"Shit," said a few of them at once.

They all had their rifles up and ready. Everyone except Sadie. She was too stunned to raise her gun. She'd known not to hope, but she'd let it get the best of her, and now... now she was beyond devastated.

"What's the plan, Mandy?" said Chad.

"Shit if I know," said Mandy.

"Shoot to kill," said James. "Shoot as soon as they get out."

They spoke tensely, knowing that they might have finally found their last living moments.

The Bronco stopped. It was close to them, but Sadie couldn't see through the windshield. She just saw shadows and reflections playing across it.

The door opened.

"Don't shoot!"

"It was a familiar voice. Impossibly familiar.

It was her mom.

Alive.

Sadie dropped her gun and ran towards her mother, tears streaming down her face.

"Mom!" cried Sadie.

There were tears in her mom's eyes as Sadie embraced her, hugging her as tightly as she could, never wanting to let her go.

Max appeared, limping horribly. His face was black and blue, badly swollen. His nose was crooked, dried blood all over his face, poorly wiped off.

James joined in the hug, and for a moment it felt like it was just three of them in the world, their little family together once again. It was as if nothing had happened and nothing ever would happen to them again.

When Sadie finally looked up, Mandy was kissing Max, smashing her pretty face against his battered one.

All of them were laughing and crying, often at the same time.

Sadie felt good.

But she knew it wasn't over. Not yet. Maybe not ever.

"So what's the plan?" said Chad.

"Same as before," said Max. "Head west."

Sadie tried not to hope. She should have known better, but she found herself longing for a calm life, somewhere out west, in a remote spot away from the madness, where they could all start to live again, undisturbed.

ABOUT RYAN WESTFIELD

Ryan Westfield is an author of post-apocalyptic survival thrillers. He's always had an interest in "being prepared," and spends time wondering what that really means. When he's not writing and reading, he enjoys being outdoors.

Contact Ryan at ryan@ryanwestfield.com